Look for all six
Special 30th Anniversary Collectors' Editions
from some of our most popular authors.

TEMPTED BY HER INNOCENT KISS
by Maya Banks
with "Never Too Late" by Brenda Jackson

BEHIND BOARDROOM DOORS
by Jennifer Lewis
with "The Royal Cousin's Revenge"
by Catherine Mann

THE PATERNITY PROPOSITION
by Merline Lovelace
with "The Sheik's Virgin" by Susan Mallery

A TOUCH OF PERSUASION
by Janice Maynard
with "A Lover's Touch" by Brenda Jackson

A FORBIDDEN

with "F...   ...arly

C...

with "B...   ...anne Banks

* * *

Dear Reader,

Happy 30th anniversary, Desire!

It is hard to believe that Harlequin Desire is thirty years old. Time sure flies when you're having fun reading the hottest books in the publishing world. I can remember when I picked up my very first Desire, and reading it on my lunch break at work. I thought the same thing about it then that I do now. "Wow, this little red book is hot!"

Little did I know that years later I would be one of the authors writing those "hot" stories. Doing so has been both an honor and a privilege. And I remain in the ranks of readers who often say, "There's nothing like a Desire."

I have written more than twenty stories for Desire and I am honored to be sharing one of my short stories with you. "Never Too Late" is a very special story and introduced one of my favorite families—the Steeles. When two people truly love each other, nothing can tear them apart, and Dane and Sienna prove just how much that statement holds true as they find their way back to everlasting love.

Congratulations, Desire! Happy 30th anniversary! And may you have many, many more!

Brenda Jackson

MAYA BANKS

TEMPTED BY HER INNOCENT KISS

ISBN-13: 978-0-373-73156-5

TEMPTED BY HER INNOCENT KISS

Copyright © 2012 by Harlequin Books S.A.

The publisher acknowledges the copyright holders
of the individual works as follows:

TEMPTED BY HER INNOCENT KISS
Copyright © 2012 by Maya Banks

NEVER TOO LATE
Copyright © 2006 by Harlequin Books S.A.
Brenda Jackson is acknowledged as the author of this work.

Recycling programs
for this product may
not exist in your area.

CONTENTS

Books by Maya Banks

Harlequin Desire

†*Enticed by His Forgotten Lover* #2107
†*Wanted by Her Lost Love* #2119
†*Tempted by Her Innocent Kiss* #2143

Silhouette Desire

*The Tycoon's Pregnant Mistress #1920
*The Tycoon's Rebel Bride #1944
*The Tycoon's Secret Affair #1960
Billionaire's Contract Engagement #2001

*The Anetakis Tycoons
†Pregnancy & Passion

Other titles by this author available in ebook format.

MAYA BANKS

has loved romance novels from a very (very) early age, and almost from the start, she dreamed of writing them, as well. In her teens she filled countless notebooks with overdramatic stories of love and passion. Today her stories are only slightly less dramatic, but no less romantic.

She lives in Texas with her husband and three children and wouldn't contemplate living anywhere other than the South. When she's not writing, she's usually hunting, fishing or playing poker. She loves to hear from her readers, and she can be found on Facebook or you can follow her on Twitter (@maya_banks). Her website, www.mayabanks.com, is where you can find up-to-date information on all of Maya's current and upcoming releases.

Dear Reader,

This month marks the thirtieth anniversary of the Desire romance line, and I'm thrilled that my book will be part of that celebration! Harlequin has always given me some of my favorite stories over the years, dating back to when I was quite a young girl reading my very first romances. That I'm now writing for a line that has brought me so much enjoyment gives me more satisfaction than I can possibly describe.

Tempted by Her Innocent Kiss is the third book in my Pregnancy & Passion miniseries and is quite possibly my favorite of the series. Devon is well caught and has resigned himself to the fact that marriage to Ashley Copeland is his only option. He accepts his fate with good grace, but he makes the mistake of trying to change who and what Ashley is.

Ashley is a wonderful heroine, one of my favorite I've ever written. She's strong, resilient and she refuses to change in the end because she *likes* who and what she is. And she demands that Devon love her for who she is.

I hope you'll enjoy *Tempted by Her Innocent Kiss* and will look forward to the final book in the miniseries, *Undone by Her Tender Touch,* coming in May!

Love,

Maya

For Dee and Lillie

TEMPTED BY HER INNOCENT KISS

Maya Banks

One

There came a time in a man's life when he knew he was well and truly caught. Devon Carter stared down at the brilliant diamond solitaire ring nestled in velvet and acknowledged that this was one such time. He snapped the lid closed and shoved the box into the breast pocket of his suit.

He had two choices. He could marry Ashley Copeland and fulfill his goal of merging his company with Copeland Hotels, thus creating the largest, most exclusive line of resorts in the world, or he could refuse and lose it all.

Put in that light, there wasn't much he could do except pop the question.

The doorman to his Manhattan high-rise hurried to open the door as Devon strode toward the street, where his driver waited. He took a deep breath before ducking into the car, and the driver pulled into traffic.

Tonight was the night. All of his careful wooing—the countless dinners, kisses that started brief and casual and became more breathless—was a lead-up to tonight. Tonight his seduction of Ashley Copeland would be complete, and then he'd ask her to marry him.

He shook his head as the absurdity of the situation hit him for the hundredth time. Personally he thought William Copeland was crazy for forcing his daughter down Devon's throat. He'd tried everything to sway the older man from his aim to see his daughter married off...to Devon.

Ashley was a sweet enough girl, but Devon had no desire to marry anyone. Not yet. Maybe in five years. Then he'd select a wife, have two-point-five children and have it all.

William had other plans. From the moment Devon had approached him, William held a calculated gleam in his eye. He'd told Devon that Ashley had no head for business. She was too soft-hearted, too naive, too...everything to ever take an active role in the family business. He was convinced that any man who showed interest in her would only be seeking to ingratiate himself into the Copeland fold—and the fortune that went with her. William wanted her taken care of and for whatever reason, he thought Devon was the best choice.

And so he'd made Ashley part and parcel of the deal. The catch? Ashley wasn't to learn of it. The old man might be willing to barter his daughter, but he damn sure didn't want her to know about it. Which meant that Devon was stuck playing stupid games. He winced at the things he'd said, the patience he'd exerted in his courting of Ashley. He was a blunt, straight-forward person, and this whole mess made him grit his teeth.

If she was part of the deal, he'd rather all parties know that from the outset so there would be no misunderstandings, no hurt feelings and no misconceptions.

Ashley was going to think this was a grand love match. She was a starry-eyed, soft-hearted woman who preferred to spend time with her animal rescue foundation over board meetings, charts and financials for Copeland Hotels.

If she ever found out the truth, she wasn't going to take it well. And hell, he couldn't blame her. Devon hated manipulation, and he'd be pissed if someone was doing to him what he was doing to her.

"Stupid old fool," Devon muttered.

His driver pulled up to the apartment building that was home to the entire Copeland clan. William and his wife occupied a penthouse on the top floor, but Ashley had moved to a smaller apartment on a lower floor. Various other family members, from cousins to aunts and uncles, lived in all places in between.

The Copeland family was an anomaly to Devon. He'd been on his own since he was eighteen, and the only thing he remembered of his parents was the occasional reminder not to "screw up."

All this devotion William showered on his children was alien and it made Devon uncomfortable. Especially since William seemed determined to treat Devon like a son now that he was marrying Ashley.

Devon started to get out when he saw Ashley fly through the door, a wide smile on her face, her eyes sparkling as she saw him.

What the hell?

He hurried toward her, a frown on his face.

"Ashley, you should have stayed inside. I would have come for you."

In response, she laughed, the sound vibrant and fresh among the sounds of traffic. Her long blond hair hung free tonight instead of being pulled up by a clip in her usual careless manner. She reached for his hands and squeezed as she smiled up at him.

"Really, Devon, what could happen to me? Alex is right here, and he watches over me worse than my father does."

Alex, the doorman, smiled indulgently in Ashley's direction. It was a smile most people wore around her. Patient, somewhat bemused, but nearly everyone who met her was enchanted by her effervescence.

Devon sighed and pulled Ashley's hands up to his waist. "You should wait inside where it's safe and let me come in for you. Alex can't protect you. He has other duties to attend to."

Her eyes sparkled merrily, and she flung her arms around his neck, startling him with the unexpected show of affection.

"That's what you're for, silly. I can't imagine anyone ever hurting me when you're around."

Before he could respond, she fused her lips hungrily to his. For God's sake the woman had no sense of self-control. She was making a spectacle here in the doorway to her apartment building.

Still, his body reacted to the hunger in her kiss. She tasted sweet and so damn innocent. He felt like an ogre for the deception he was carrying out.

But then he remembered that Copeland Hotels would finally be his—or at least under his control. He would be a force to be reckoned with worldwide. Not bad for a man who had been told that his sole ambition should be not to "screw up."

Carefully, he pulled her away and gently offered a reprimand.

"This isn't the place, Ashley. We should be going. Carl is waiting for us."

Her lips turned down into a momentary frown before she looked beyond him to Carl, and once again she rushed forward, a bright smile on her face.

He shook his head as she greeted his chauffeur, her hands flying everywhere as she spoke in rapid tones. Carl grinned. The man actually *grinned* as he handed Ashley into the car. By the time Devon made it over, Carl had already reverted back to his somber countenance.

Devon slid into the backseat with Ashley, and she immediately moved over to nestle into his side.

"Where are we eating tonight?" she asked.

"I planned something special."

As expected she all but pounced on him, her eyes shining with excitement.

"What?" she demanded.

He smiled. "You'll see."

He felt more than heard her faint huff of exasperation and his smile broadened. One thing in Ashley's favor was that she was extraordinarily easy to please. He was unused to women who didn't wheedle, pout or complain when their expectations weren't met. And unfortunately, the women he usually spent time with had high expectations. *Expensive* expectations. Ashley seemed happy no matter what he presented her with. He had every confidence that the ring he'd chosen would meet with her approval.

She nestled closer to him and laid her head on his shoulder. Her spontaneous demonstrations of affection still unbalanced him. He wasn't used to people who were so…unreserved.

William Copeland felt that Ashley needed someone who understood and accepted her nature. Why he thought Devon fit the bill Devon would never know.

When they married, he would work on getting her to restrain some of her enthusiasm. She couldn't go through her entire life with her emotions on her sleeve. It would only get her hurt.

A few minutes later, Carl pulled up to Devon's building and got out to open the door. Devon stepped out and then extended his hand to help Ashley from the car.

Her brow was creased in a thoughtful expression as she stared up at the building.

"This is your place."

He chuckled at her statement of the obvious. "So it is. Come, our dinner awaits."

He ushered her through the open door and into a waiting elevator. It soared to the top and opened into the foyer of his apartment. To his satisfaction, everything was just as he'd arranged.

The lighting was low and romantic. Soft jazz played in the background and the table by the window overlooking the city had been set for two.

"Oh, Devon, this is perfect!"

Once again she threw herself into his arms and gave him a squeeze worthy of someone much larger than herself. It did funny things to his chest every time she hugged him.

Extricating himself from her hold, he guided her toward the table. He pulled her chair out for her and then reached for a bottle of wine to pour them both a glass.

"The food is still hot!" she exclaimed as she touched the plate in front of her. "How did you manage it?"

He chuckled. "My super powers?"

"Mmm, I like the idea of a man with super cooking powers."

"I had someone in while I was gone to collect you."

She wrinkled her nose. "You're horribly old-fashioned, Dev. There was no reason to collect me if we were spending the evening at your apartment. I could have gotten a cab or had my father's driver run me over."

He blinked in surprise. Old-fashioned? He'd been accused of a lot of things, but never of being old-fashioned. Then he scowled.

"A man should see to his woman's needs. All of them. It was my pleasure to pick you up."

Her cheeks pinkened in the candlelight, and her eyes shone like he'd just handed her the keys to a brand-new car.

"Am I?" she asked huskily.

He cocked his head to the side as he set his wineglass down. "Are you what?"

"Your woman."

Something unfurled inside him. He wouldn't have considered himself a possessive man, but now that he'd decided that she would be his wife, he discovered he felt very possessive where she was concerned.

"Yes," he said softly. "And before the night is over, you'll have no doubts that you belong to me."

A full body shiver took over Ashley. How was she supposed to concentrate on dinner after a statement like that? Devon stared at her across the table like he was going to pounce at any moment.

He had the most arresting eyes. Not really brown, but a warm shade of amber. In the sunlight they looked golden and in the candlelight they looked like a mountain lion's. She felt like prey, but it was a delicious feeling, not at all threatening. She'd been waiting for the moment when Devon would take their relationship a step further.

She'd longed for it and dreaded it with equal intensity. How could she possibly keep pace with a man who could seduce a woman with nothing more than a touch and a glance?

He'd been a consummate gentleman during the time they'd been dating. At first he'd only given her gentle, nonthreatening kisses, but over time they'd become more passionate and she'd gotten a glimpse of the powerfully sensual man under the protective armor.

She had a feeling that once those layers were peeled back, the man behind them was ferocious, possessive and…savage.

Another shiver overtook her at the direction of her thoughts. They were fanciful, yes, but she truly believed her assessment. Would she find out tonight? Did he plan to make her his?

"Aren't you going to eat?" Devon prompted.

She stared down at her plate again. What was it anyway? She wasn't sure she could eat a bite. Her mouth felt as if it was full of sawdust, and her entire body trembled with anticipation.

She moved the shrimp with her fork so that it gathered some of the sauce and slowly raised it to her lips.

"You aren't a vegetarian, are you?"

She laughed at the look on his face, as if the idea had just occurred to him.

"Tell me I haven't been serving you food you won't eat all

this time," Devon said with a grimace. "You would have said something, wouldn't you have?"

She put the shrimp into her mouth and chewed as she put the fork down. When she'd swallowed she reached over to touch his hand.

"You worry too much. I would have told you if I was a vegetarian. A lot of people assume since I'm so active in my animal rescue organization that I refuse to eat meat of any kind."

The relief on his face made her laugh again.

"I'll eat chicken and most seafood. I'm not crazy about pork or the more uppity stuff like veal, foie gras and stuff like that."

A shudder worked over her shoulders.

"There's something about eating duck liver that just turns my stomach."

Devon chuckled. "It's actually quite good. Have you tried it?"

She wrinkled her nose in distaste. "Sorry. I have a thing about eating any sort of innard."

"Ah, so no cow's tongue for you then."

She held up her hands and shook her head back and forth. "Don't say it. Just don't say it. That's beyond disgusting."

"I'll make a note of your food preferences so that I never serve you animal guts," he said solemnly.

She grinned over at him. "You know, Devon, you're not as stiff as everyone thinks you are. You actually have quite a sense of humor."

One finely arched eyebrow shot upward. "Stiff? Who thinks I'm stiff?"

Realizing she'd put her foot solidly in her mouth, she stuffed another shrimp in to keep the foot company.

"Nobody," she mumbled around her food. "Forget I said anything."

"Has someone been warning you off of me?"

The sudden tension in his voice sent a prickle of unease over her.

"My family worries for me," she said simply. "They're very protective. Too protective," she finished with a mutter.

"Your *family* is warning you about me?"

He acted as though it was the very last thing he expected. Was he so sure that her entire family was pushing for a match between them?

"Well no, not exactly. Definitely not Daddy. He thinks you hung the moon. Mama approves but I'm sure it's because Daddy does. She thinks he can do nothing wrong so if you have his stamp of approval you have hers."

He seemed to relax in his chair. "Who then?"

She shrugged. "My brother wants me to be careful, but you have to understand he's been saying the same thing about all the guys I've ever dated."

Again that eyebrow went up as he raised the glass of wine to his lips. "Oh?"

"Yeah, you know, you're a philanderer, a player. Different woman on your arm every week. You aren't serious. You just want to get me into bed."

A blast of heat surged into her cheeks and she ducked her head. Stupid thing to blurt out. Stupid!

"Sounds like a typical older brother," Devon said blandly. "But he's right about one thing. I do want you in my bed. The difference is, once you're there, you're going to stay."

Her lips popped into an *O*.

He smiled, a lazy, self-assured smile that oozed male confidence.

"Finish eating, Ashley. I want you to enjoy your meal. We'll enjoy…each other…later."

She ate mechanically. She didn't register the taste. For all she knew she *was* eating cow's tongue.

What did women do in situations like these? Here was a man obviously determined to take her to bed. Did she play it cool? Did she go on the offensive? Did she offer to undress for him?

A bubble of laughter bounced into her throat. Oh, Lord, but she was in way over her head.

Firm hands rested on her shoulders and squeezed reassuringly. She yanked her head up to see Devon behind her. How had he gotten there?

"Relax, Ash," he said gently. "You're wound tighter than a spring. Come here."

On shaking legs, she rose to stand in front of him. He touched her cheek with one finger then raised it to her temple to push at a tendril of her hair. He traced a line over her face and down to her lips before finally moving in, his body crowding hers.

He wrapped one arm around her waist, and cupped her nape with his other hand. This time when he kissed her there was none of the restraint she'd seen in the past. It was like kissing an inferno.

Hot, breathless, so overwhelming that her senses shattered. How could one kiss do this to her?

His tongue brushed over her lips, softly at first and then more firmly as he forced her mouth to open under his gentle pressure.

She relaxed and melted into his embrace. Her body hummed. Her pulse thudded against her temples, at her neck and deep in her body at her very core. She wanted this man. Sometimes she felt like she'd been waiting for him forever. He was so…right.

"Devon," she whispered.

He pushed far enough away that he could see her, but he still held her firm in his embrace.

"Yes, sweetheart?"

Her heart fluttered at the endearment.

"There's something I need to tell you. Something you should know."

His brow furrowed, and he searched her eyes as if gauging her mood.

"Go ahead. You can tell me anything."

She swallowed but felt the knot grow bigger in her throat. She hadn't imagined it being this difficult to say, but she felt suddenly silly. Maybe she shouldn't say anything at all. Maybe she should just let things happen. But no, this was a special night. It needed to be special. He deserved to know.

"I—I've never done this." She gripped his upper arm with nervous fingers. "What I mean is that I've never made love with a man before. You…you'd be the first."

Something dark and primitive sparked in his eyes. His grip tightened around her waist. At first he didn't say anything. He kissed her hungrily, his lips devouring hers.

Then he pulled away, savage satisfaction written on every facet of his face.

"I'm glad. After tonight you'll be mine, Ashley. I'm glad I'm the first."

"Me, too," she whispered.

Some of the fierceness in his expression eased. He leaned forward and kissed her on the brow and held his lips there for a long moment.

His hands ran soothingly up and down her arms, stopping to squeeze her shoulders. "I don't want you to be afraid. I'll be very gentle with you, sweetheart. I'll make sure you enjoy every moment of it."

She reached up on tiptoe to wrap both arms around his neck. "Then make love to me, Devon. I've waited so long for you."

Two

Ashley stared up at Devon, unsure of what to do now. He didn't suffer any such problem. Dropping another kiss on her brow, he bent and lifted her into his arms and carried her to the large master bedroom in the corner of the apartment.

She sighed as she laid her head on his chest. "I've always dreamed of being carried to bed when the big moment came. I probably sound silly."

Soft laughter rumbled from his chest. "Glad I could fulfill one of your fantasies before I even get you naked."

She blushed but felt a giddy thrill at the idea of him undressing her. That was number two on her fantasy list for when she lost her virginity.

After listening to so many girls in high school and college talk about how utterly unremarkable their first times were, Ashley had vowed that her experience would be different. Perhaps she'd been too picky as a result, but she'd been determined to choose the right man and the right moment. So she was feeling pretty damn smug because it didn't get any more perfect than Devon Carter right here, right now.

He set her down just inside the doorway and she glanced nervously around his enormous bedroom. A person could get swallowed up in here. And the bed was equally huge. It looked custom-made. Who needed a bed that big anyway? Unless he regularly hosted orgies and slept with ten women.

"I'm going to undress you, sweetheart," he said in a husky voice. "I'll go slow and you stop me if you feel uncomfortable at any time. We have all night. There's no rush."

Her heart melted at the tenderness in his voice. He seemed so patient, and she warred with appreciating this unerringly patient side of him and being frustrated because she wanted to be ravished.

It's your first time only once.

She could hear herself issue the reprimand. And she was right. She had plenty of time for down-and-dirty, hot monkey sex. But she would only have this night once and she wanted it to be a night she'd always remember.

"Turn around so I can unzip your dress."

Slowly she turned and closed her eyes when he gently moved her hair over one shoulder so he could reach the zip. A moment later, the light rasp of the zipper filled the room and the dress loosened precariously around her bust.

She slapped her hands over the strapless neckline just before it took the plunge down her body.

Devon's hands closed around her bare shoulders and he kissed the curve of her neck. "Relax."

Easy for him to say. He'd probably done this a hundred times. That thought depressed her and she made herself swear not to dwell on how many bed partners he may have had.

He turned her back around, his smile tender enough to melt her insides. Carefully he pried her fingers away from their death grip on her dress until it fell down her body, leaving her in only her panties.

She flushed scarlet. Why, oh, why hadn't she just worn the strapless bra? She felt like a hussy for not wearing anything but it wasn't as if she had a huge amount of cleavage and the dress fit tightly over her chest so she hadn't been in danger of flopping out of it.

And it wasn't as if she knew she was going to be seduced tonight.

She'd hoped. But then she'd hoped every time Devon took her out. She'd given up on trying to predict when or if the day might come.

"Very sexy," Devon breathed out as his gaze raked up and down her body.

Thank goodness she'd worn the lacy, sexy panties and not the plain white cotton ones she sometimes wore when she was feeling particularly uninspired or just didn't give a damn whether she felt girly and pretty or not.

"You're beautiful, Ash. So damn beautiful."

Some of her trembling stopped as she absorbed the look in his eyes. The eyes didn't lie and she could read arousal and appreciation in those golden depths.

He took her shoulders, gently pulled her to him and kissed her again. Hot. Forceful. In turns fierce and then gentler as though he had to remind himself not to overwhelm her.

She wanted to be overwhelmed.

She may be a virgin but she was no stranger to lust, desire and extreme arousal. She wanted Devon with a force that bordered on obsession. He'd fired many a fantasy that had kept her up at night.

And it wasn't as if she hadn't been tempted in the past. She'd been courted by other men. Some she felt absolutely no desire for but with others she'd experienced a kernel of interest and had wondered if she should pursue a sexual relationship. In the end, she hadn't been sure and if she wasn't absolutely sure, she'd promised herself she wouldn't take the plunge.

Not so with Devon. She'd known from the moment he introduced himself to her in that husky, sexy-as-hell voice that she was a goner. She'd spent the last weeks breathless in anticipation of this night. Now that it was here, her entire body ached for him to take her.

He pulled away for a moment and she stared at him with glazed eyes. He touched her cheek, tracing a path down her face with his fingertip. Then he kissed her again. And again.

Hot. Breathless. His tongue slid between her lips and feathered over her own. Warm and decadent, his taste seeped over her tongue and she drank him in hungrily, wanting more.

His harsh groan exploded into her mouth and the rush of his exhalation blew over her face. "You make me crazy."

She smiled, some of her nervousness abating. That she had this effect on this gorgeous, perfect man infused her with a sudden rush of feminine confidence.

He fastened his mouth to her jaw and kissed a line down to her neck. He pressed his lips just over her pulse point and then lightly grazed his teeth over the sensitive flesh.

Shivers of delight danced over her shoulders. His hands glided up her arms and then gripped her just above the elbows. He held her in place as his mouth continued its downward trek. Over the curve of her shoulder and then down the front.

He went to his knees in front of her so that his mouth was barely an inch from her nipple. She sucked in her breath, afraid to move, wanting so badly for him to touch her there. His mouth, lips, tongue... She didn't care. She just knew she'd die if he didn't touch her.

He lowered his head and kissed her belly instead. Just above her navel. She sucked in her breath, causing her stomach to cave in. He moved up an inch and kissed her again, tracing a path between her breasts until finally he pressed a kiss directly over where her heart beat.

A slow smile turned his lips upward, the movement light against her skin.

"Your heart's racing," he murmured.

She remained silent. It didn't require acknowledgement from her—her heart *was* beyond racing. It was damn near about to explode out of her chest.

But her hands wouldn't remain still. Drawn to the light brown wash of his hair, she threaded her fingers through the short strands. In a certain light, she could see the shades of his eyes. Amber. Golden. That warm, liquid brown.

Her fingers moved easily through his hair. No styling products stiffened the strands. A little mussed. Never quite the same from day to day. He paid as little attention to his hair as he did to the other things he deemed inconsequential.

He glanced up, her fingers still thrust into his hair. "Are you afraid?"

"Terrified," she admitted.

His gaze softened and he wrapped his arms around her body, pulling her into his embrace. The shock of her naked body against his still fully clothed one sent shivers up her spine.

"I'd feel less afraid if you were naked, though."

He blinked in surprise and then he threw back his head and laughed. "You little tease." He pushed upward to his feet until he towered over her. "I'm happy to accommodate you. *More* than happy to accommodate you."

She licked over suddenly dry lips as he pulled away and began unbuttoning his shirt. He tugged the ends from his slacks and unfastened his cuffs before shrugging out of the sleeves.

She swayed precariously because oh, Lord, was the man mouthwateringly gorgeous. He was lean in an "I work out" way but he wasn't so muscled that he looked like he got carried away with the fitness regimen. He was hard in all the right places without being a neckless, snarling, swollen, knuckles-dragging-the-ground caveman type.

A smattering of light brown hair collected in a whorl in the center of his chest and then tapered to a fine line that drifted down his abdomen and disappeared into the waist of his pants.

She wanted to touch him. Had to touch him. She curled her fingers until they dug into her palms and then she frowned. There weren't rules to seduction, right? She could touch. No reason for her to stand here like a statue or an automaton while he did all the work. While taking things slow did have its good points, there was simply too much she wanted to experience to stand idly by while seduction *happened*. She wanted to take an active part.

He'd only began to undo his pants, when she slid her hands over his chest and up to his shoulders. He went still and for a moment closed his eyes.

His response fascinated her. Did her touch bring him as much pleasure as his touch brought her? A sudden rush of power bolted through her veins, awakening the feminine roar inside her.

She moved in closer, wanting to feel his naked flesh against hers. Hot. She gasped when her breasts pressed against his chest. It was an electric sensation that was wildly intoxicating. She wanted more. So much more.

"What are you doing?" he asked hoarsely.

"Enjoying myself."

He smiled at that and remained still, his hands still gripping the fly of his pants. She ran her palms openly over his chest, exploring each muscled ridge, enjoying the rugged contrast between his hardness and the softness of her own body.

"Take them off," she whispered when her hands drifted perilously close to where his hands were positioned.

"Has the blushing virgin turned temptress?"

On cue, she flushed but he smiled and then let go of his pants to frame her face in his palms. He kissed her, nearly scorching her lips off with the sudden heat. "You take them off me," he murmured into her mouth.

Sudden nerves made her fingers clumsy as she fumbled

with his pants, but he stood there patiently, his hands caressing her face, gaze locked with hers as she pushed his pants down his legs.

Swallowing, she chanced a look down to see his erection straining hard against the cotton of his briefs. Plain, boxer briefs. Somehow she'd imagined something a little more... She wasn't sure. She just knew she hadn't imagined plain boxer briefs but then he was a no-fuss kind of guy. Yes, he wore expensive clothing, but it was comfortable expensive clothing. The kind you only knew was expensive because you recognized the label. Not because it looked terribly pricey.

Simply put, Devon Carter looked like a man who'd made money but wasn't overly concerned with appearing as though he was wealthy. It wasn't as if he couldn't look the part. She'd seen him in full business attire with the sleek designer labels and the polished, arrogant look to match. But she'd spent much more time with him privately. When he was relaxed. Less guarded. That was the word. In public situations, he was intensely guarded at all times. Almost as if he was determined to let no one in. It thrilled her that he trusted her enough to see his more casual side.

"Put your hand around me," he coaxed in that low husky tone that had her melting.

Tentatively she slid her fingers beyond the waistband of his underwear and delved lower until she encountered the velvety hardness of his erection. Emboldened by the immediate darkening of his eyes, she curled her fingers around the base and slowly slid upward, lightly skimming along his length.

His hands left her face and he impatiently pushed his underwear down until he was completely nude, cupped in her hands as she gently caressed him.

Having nothing but stolen glimpses of elicit photos to compare him to, he seemed to measure up adequately in the size department. At least he didn't look so huge that she feared compatibility issues.

He gently took her wrists and pulled her hands away from his erection. Then he pulled her hands up until they were trapped between them against his chest. His thumb lightly caressed the inside of her palm as he stared into her eyes.

"You, my love, are driving me slowly insane. It was me who was supposed to do the seducing and yet you utterly enslave me with every touch."

She flushed with pleasure, her skin growing warm under the intense desire blazing in his eyes.

He kissed her again, and he pressed in close until he walked her backward toward the bed. He stopped when the backs of her legs brushed against the sumptuous comforter.

He wrapped his arm around her waist and lowered her back until she was lying on the mattress, him hovering above her.

His expression grew serious and he brushed her hair from her forehead in a tender gesture. "If at any time I do something that frightens you, tell me and I'll stop. If at any time you simply want to slow down, just let me know."

"Oh," she breathed out. Because it was impossible to say anything else around the tightness in her throat.

She reached for him, pulled him down to meet her kiss. She felt clumsy and inept but it didn't seem to matter to him. She wished she was more artful. More practiced. But she couldn't wish for experience because more than anything she was glad she'd waited for this moment. For him.

"I love you," she whispered, unable to hold back the words that swelled and finally broke free.

He went still and for a moment she was terrified that she'd effectively thrown a wet blanket over a fire. She drew away, eyes wide as she searched his face for something. Some reaction. Some indication that she'd breached some forbidden barrier.

Trust her to ruin what would have been the most exciting, wonderful, splendiferous moment of her life by opening her big mouth. She'd never been able to restrain herself. She tried. Most of the time.

"Devon?"

His name came out in a near croak. Her lips shook and she started to withdraw, already feeling the heat of embarrassment lick over her with painful precision.

Instead of answering her, he moved over her in a powerful rush. He took her mouth roughly, devouring her lips as his tongue plunged inside, tangling with hers.

Her body surged to life, arching up into his. She wrapped her arms around his neck as he gathered her tightly against him. Their bodies were as fused as their mouths. Between her legs, she could feel him so hard. Hot.

His hips jerked, almost as if he could barely contain the urge to push inside her. She gasped for air, partly out of excitement, partly out of sudden, delicious fear and anticipation.

His hands and mouth were everywhere. A sensual assault on her senses. Magic. Gentle caresses mixed with firmer, rougher touches. He slid down her body until his mouth hovered over one taut nipple. And then he flicked his tongue out and licked the tip.

She cried out, nearly undone by the shock of such a simple touch. Pleasure rocked over her and she shuddered violently, her fingers suddenly digging into his flesh, marking him.

Not satisfied with the intensity of her reaction, he closed his mouth over the rigid peak and sucked strongly.

Her vision blurred. She gasped but couldn't seem to draw air into her lungs. Oh, but it was heaven. So edgy. She couldn't even find the words to describe such a decadent sensation as his mouth sucking at her breast.

But then his hand slid between them, over the softness of her belly and lower.

She held her breath as his fingers tentatively brushed through her sensitive folds and then he found her heat, teasing, touching. He knew better than she knew herself exactly how to pleasure her. Where to touch her. *How* to touch her. Each stroke brought her to greater heights.

It was as though she was being wound tighter and tighter. Tension coiled in her belly. Low. Humming through her pelvis. She wasn't ignorant of orgasms, but this was nothing like she'd ever experienced before. It was powerful. Relentless. Nearly frightening in its intensity.

His fingers left her and he carefully parted her legs. His hand glided soothingly up the inside of her thigh and then he stroked her intimately again as he positioned himself above her.

His mouth left her breasts and she moaned her protest. He covered her lips once more with his own and then whispered softly to her.

"Hold on to me, love. Touch me. I'm going to go inside you now. I'll be gentle. There's nothing to be afraid of."

She trembled from head to toe. Not in fear or trepidation. She was so close to release that she feared the moment he pushed inside her the barest inch that she'd go over the edge, and she wanted it to last. She wanted to enjoy every single moment of what was to come.

"Wait," she choked out.

He went still, the tip of his erection just touching the mouth of her opening. Strain was evident in his face as he stared down at her, but he held himself in check.

"Are you all right? Did I frighten you?" he asked urgently.

She shook her head. "No. No, I'm fine. I just needed a second. I'm so close. Just need to catch up."

He smiled then, his eyes gleaming with a predatory light. "Tell me when."

She reached up once more, feathering her hands over his shoulders and to the bunched muscles of his back. Her gaze met his and she drowned in those beautiful amber eyes. "When."

He swallowed hard and his lips tightened into a harsh line.

Then he closed his eyes and flexed his hips, pushing into her inch by delicious inch.

At one point he stopped and she stirred restlessly, a protest forming.

"Shh," he murmured as he kissed the corner of her mouth. "Give me just a moment. I don't want to hurt you. Better to have done with it quickly."

She nodded her agreement just as he surged forward, burying himself to the hilt.

Her eyes widened and a strangled sound escaped her throat as she sought to process the sudden wash of conflicting sensations that bombarded her from every angle.

He was deep. Impossibly deep. She surrounded him. He surrounded her. Their hips were flush against each other. His body covered hers possessively. There was a burning ache deep inside her, and she couldn't discern whether it was pleasure or pain.

She just knew she wanted—needed—more.

She whimpered lightly and struggled, not against him, not in protest. She wanted something she couldn't name. She wanted…him. All of him.

"Easy," he soothed.

He kissed her, stroked his tongue over hers and then deepened the kiss just as he began to move inside her. Gently. He was so gentle and reverent. He lifted his body off of her and arched his hips, pushing deep then retreating.

Then he levered himself down, resting on his forearms, never breaking away from her eyes.

"Okay?"

She smiled. "Very okay."

"You're beautiful, Ash. So very beautiful. So innocent and perfect and mine."

His. The possessive growl in his voice thrilled her and sent another cascade of pleasure through her body.

"Yes, yours," she whispered.

"Tell me how close you are. I want to make sure you're with me. I can't hold off much longer."

"Then don't." Her voice shook. She was nearly beyond the ability to think much less speak. Her body was taut. Her senses were shattered and she was so very close to losing all control. Just one touch. One more touch…

He gathered her close and thrust again. And then again. He forced her thighs farther apart, plunged deeper and she lost all sense of herself.

She cried out his name. Heard him murmur close to her ear. Soothing. Comforting. Telling her beautiful things she could barely make sense of. She was spiraling at a dizzying speed, faster and faster until she closed her eyes.

It was the single most beautiful, spectacular sensation she could imagine. She'd wanted wonderful, but this far surpassed even her most erotic fantasies.

When she regained at least a modicum of sanity, she was firmly wrapped in Devon's embrace and his mouth was moving lightly over her neck. For that matter she was on top of him. Her hair was flung to one side while he nuzzled at the curve of her shoulder, moving up and down to just below her ear and back to her shoulder.

She raised her head to stare down at him, still feeling a little fuzzy around the edges. "How did I get here?"

He smiled and slid his hands over her naked body. They stopped at her behind and he squeezed affectionately. "I put you here. I like you covering me. I could get used to it."

"Oh."

He raised one eyebrow. "Speechless? You?"

She sent him a disgruntled look but was too wasted to follow up with any sort of admonishment. Okay, so obviously she was speechless.

He chuckled and pulled her down against him. She settled over him with a sigh and he rubbed his palm over her back, stroking and caressing as she lay draped over him like a wet noodle.

"Did I hurt you?"

She smiled at the concern in his voice. "No. It was perfect, Dev. So perfect I can't even find the words to describe it. Thank you."

He lifted a strand of hair and lazily twined his fingers around it. "Thank you? I don't think I've ever been thanked by a woman after sex."

"You made my first time special," she said quietly. "It was perfect. You were perfect."

He kissed the top of her head. "I'm glad."

She yawned against his chest and cuddled deeper into his hold.

"Go to sleep," he murmured. "I want you to sleep here tonight."

Her eyes were incredibly heavy, and she was already drifting off when his directive registered in her consciousness.

"Want to sleep here, too," she mumbled.

His fingers stilled in her hair and then his hands wandered down her body, bold and possessive. "That's good, Ash, because from now on, you'll sleep every night in my bed."

Three

Devon woke to the odd sensation of a female body wrapped around him. Not just wrapped but completely and utterly surrounding him.

Ashley was draped across him, her legs tangled with his, her breasts flattened against his chest, her arm thrown across his body and her face burrowed into his neck.

He...liked it.

He lay there a long while watching the soft rise and fall of her body as she slept soundly across him. She was really quite beautiful in an unsophisticated, effervescent way. She lit up a room when she walked in. You could always pick her out of a crowd. She was extremely...natural. Perhaps a bit too exuberant and unrestrained but in time with the proper guidance, she'd be an excellent wife and mother.

He ran the tips of his finger lightly up her arm. She was pale. Not so pale she looked unhealthy, but it was obvious she wasn't a sun bunny, nor did she indulge in salon tanning. Perhaps what he liked most about her was that she looked the same no matter when he saw her. Though she wore makeup, she didn't wear so much that she was transformed into someone completely different when they went out.

Glossy lips and a touch of coal to already long, lush lashes seemed to be all she did, but then he was hardly an expert on women's gunk.

But she didn't seem fake. At least not that he could tell. Yet. Who knew what the future would bring. He liked to think she wasn't an accomplice in this ridiculous plan of her father's even when he knew it was best for all parties involved to know the entire story from the start.

The selfish bastard in him liked the idea that she felt affection for him, free of machinations. If her words from the night before weren't merely a result of being overwhelmed in the moment, *affection* was perhaps the wrong term. She'd said she loved him.

It both complicated the matter and gave him a certain amount of satisfaction.

While he may approach the marriage as a matter of necessity, convenience and a chance at a successful business venture, the idea that she would be coming into the marriage for the same reasons bothered him immensely.

It made him a flaming hypocrite but he was happy for her to want him because she desired him and yes, even loved him.

First, however, he had to get the preliminaries out of the way. One of which was making their upcoming nuptials official. She didn't know it yet, but she would become Mrs. Devon Carter.

He carefully extricated himself from the tangle of arms and legs, but he needn't have worried because she slept soundly, only wrinkling her nose and mumbling something in her sleep when he slipped away completely.

He pulled on his robe and glanced back at the bed. For a moment he was transfixed by the image she presented. The sun streamed through the window across the room and bathed her in its warm glow.

Her blond hair was tousled and spread out over his pillow. One arm shielded most of her breasts from view, but there, just below her elbow, one nipple peeked out. The sheet slid to just over her buttocks but bared the dimple just below the small of her back.

She was indeed beautiful. And now she was his.

He dug into the pocket of the jacket he'd discarded the night before to retrieve the box with the ring in it and then quietly left the room. When she awoke, he'd put into place the next part of his carefully orchestrated plan.

Ashley stirred and stretched lazily, blinking when the sun momentarily blinded her. She kept her eyes shut for a moment, simply enjoying the warmth and comfort of the sumptuous bed. Devon's bed.

She sighed in contentment. As virginal deflowering went, that had to top the list of all-time most awesome. How could it possibly have been any better? A wonderful night. Romantic dinner for two. Devon staring at her with those gorgeous eyes and murmuring that she would now be his. Oh, yeah, perfect.

Then she realized that he was no longer in bed with her and she opened her eyes with a frown. Only to see him standing just across the room. Staring at her.

He was clad in a robe, though it dangled loosely, open just enough that she could see his bare chest. He was leaning against the doorway to the bathroom and he was simply watching her. For some reason that sent a giddy thrill up her spine.

Then a flash of color caught her eye and she glanced downward to see a lush red rose lying on the sheet next to her. But it was the tiny card propped next to a dazzling, truly spectacular diamond ring that took her breath away.

Blood rushed to her head and she stared openmouthed at the items before her. She pushed to her elbow and reached for the ring, hands shaking so badly that she was clumsy, nearly dropping the small velvet box where the ring rested.

Then she glanced at the note again, sure she'd misunderstood. But no, there it was. In his neat, distinctive scrawl.

Will you marry me?

"Oh, God," she croaked out.

She looked at the ring, looked at the note and then back up to him, almost afraid that he'd be gone and that she'd imagined this whole thing.

But he was still there, an indulgent smile carving those handsome features.

"Really?" she whispered.

He nodded and smiled more broadly. "Really."

She dropped the rose, the ring, the note—everything—and flew out of bed, across the room, and launched herself into his arms.

He stepped back and laughed as she kissed his face, his brow, his cheek and then his lips. "Yes, oh, yes! Oh, my God, Devon, yes!"

He made a grab for her behind before she could slide down him and land on the floor. Then he hoisted her up so they were eye level. "You know it's customary to actually put the ring on."

She glanced down at her hand and then over her shoulder to the bed. "Oh, my God! Where is it?"

Shaking his head, he carried her over to the bed then set her on the edge while he reached behind her.

A moment later, he took her hand and slid the diamond onto her ring finger. She sucked in her breath as the sun caught the stone and it sparkled brilliantly in the light.

"Oh, Dev, it's beautiful," she breathed.

She threw her arms around his neck and hugged him tightly. "I love you so much. I can't believe you planned all this."

He gently pulled her arms down and then collected her

hands in her lap as he stared into her eyes. "I don't want a long engagement."

Was this supposed to worry her? She beamed back at him. "Neither do I."

"In fact, I'd prefer to get married right away," he added, watching her all the while.

She frowned and chewed at her bottom lip. "I wouldn't mind. I mean if it was just me, but I don't know how my family would take that. Mama will want to plan a big wedding. I'm her only daughter. It's not that I care about a big fuss—I don't. But it would hurt her if she wasn't able to give us a big wedding."

He touched her cheek. "Leave your family to me. I assure you, they'll be on board with my plans. You and I will have the best wedding—one that your mother will be more than satisfied with. I think you'll find they won't object to our plans at all."

Excitement hurtled through her veins until it was nearly impossible to sit still. "I can't wait to tell everyone! Won't this just be amazing? Everyone will be so thrilled for me. I know Daddy despaired of me ever finding a suitable man and settling down. He always says I'm too unsettled, but really, I'm still young."

He gave her an amused smile. "Are you saying you don't want to get married?"

She stared at him in shock. "No! That's not at all what I was saying. I was merely going to say that I was waiting for the right man. In this case, you."

"That's what I like to hear," he murmured.

He leaned forward to kiss her brow. "How about you take a long bubble bath to recover from last night's activities and then we'll have breakfast together."

She flushed red. She had to be flaming. But she nodded, eager to discuss their future.

Mrs. Devon Carter. It had such a nice ring to it. And speaking of rings... She glanced down, transfixed by the radiance of the diamond that adorned her finger.

"Like it?" he asked in a teasing voice.

She looked back up at him, suddenly serious. "I love it, Dev. It's absolutely gorgeous. But you didn't need to get me something so expensive. I would have loved anything you gave me."

He smiled. "I know you would. But I wanted something special."

Her heart did a little dance in her chest. "Thank you. It's just perfect. Everything is perfect."

He kissed her again, long and leisurely. When he pulled away, his eyes were half-lidded and they were glowing with desire.

"Go draw your bath before I forget all about breakfast and make love to you again."

"Breakfast?" she whispered. "Were we planning to eat?"

He made a sound in his throat that was part growl, part resignation.

"I don't want to hurt you, Ash. As much as you tempt me, I'd rather wait until you're fully healed from last night."

She pushed out her bottom lip.

"As adorable as you are when you pout, it won't move me this time. Now get your pretty behind out of bed and hit the bathroom. Breakfast will be served in forty-five minutes. Plenty of time for you to soak."

She sighed. "Okay, okay. I'm going."

She got up and walked toward the bathroom but just as she got to the doorway, something he'd said the night before came back to her. She paused and turned around, her head cocked to the side.

"Dev, what did you mean last night when you said I'd be sleeping here with you every night from now on?"

He rose and pulled his robe tighter around his waist. He stared back at her, his gaze intense and serious.

"Exactly what I said. I'll want you to move in as soon as

possible. I'll arrange to have what you need transferred from your apartment. You're mine, Ash. From now on, you'll spend every night in my bed."

Four

"Well, you finally took the leap," Cameron Hollingsworth said as he stared across the room to where Ashley stood with a group of women.

Devon took a sip of the wine, though the taste went unappreciated. He was too distracted. Still, he forced some of it down, hoping it would at least take the edge off.

The official announcement would be made in a few moments. By Devon himself. Ashley's father had wanted to do the honors, but Devon had preferred to do it himself. William Copeland had already orchestrated entirely too much of Devon's relationship with Ashley. From now on, things would be done his way.

Though everyone in attendance was well aware it was an engagement party they had been invited to, Ashley had insisted on waiting until all the guests had arrived before their engagement was announced.

"Cold feet already?" Cam asked dryly. "You haven't said two words since I got here."

Devon grimaced. "No. It's done. No backing out now. Copeland has all but signed off on the deal. After the ceremony he'll fax the final documents and we'll move forward with the merger. I'll want to meet with you, Ryan and Rafe as soon as I return from the honeymoon."

Cam arched an eyebrow. "Honeymoon? You're actually going on one?"

"Just because this marriage is part and parcel of a business deal doesn't mean Ashley has to have any less of a marriage or honeymoon," Devon murmured.

Cam shrugged. "Good idea. Keep her happy. If she's happy, Daddy's happy. You know what they say about Daddy's girls."

Devon frowned. "Don't be an ass. She's…"

"She's what?" Cam prompted.

"Look, she has no idea what her father's done. She thinks this is a wildly romantic courtship that culminated in an equally romantic marriage proposal. If I don't take her on a honeymoon, it's going to look strange."

Cam groaned. "This can't end well. Mark my words. You're screwed, my friend."

"Anyone ever tell you what a ball of joy you are?"

Cam held his hands up in surrender. "Look, I'm just trying to warn you here. You should tell her the truth. No woman likes being made a fool of."

"And have her tell me to go to hell and take my proposal with me?" Devon demanded.

He sighed and shook his head. Yeah, he knew Cam had been through the wringer in the past. He couldn't blame his friend for his cynicism. But he wasn't in the mood to hear it right now.

"This deal is important to all of us. Not just me," he continued when Cam remained silent. "Marriage isn't my first choice, but Ash is a sweet girl. She'll make a good wife and a good mother. Everyone gets what they want. You, me, Ryan and Rafe. Ashley, her father. Everyone's happy."

"Whatever floats your boat, man. You know I'm behind you all the way. But remember this. You don't have to marry her to make this work. We'll find another company. We've suffered setbacks before. Not one of us expects you to martyr yourself for the cause. Rafe and Ryan are deliriously happy. There's no reason you shouldn't hold out for the same."

Devon snorted. "Turning into quite the rah-rah man. I'm fine, Cam. There is no love of my life. No other woman in the picture. No one I'd rather marry. I'll be content with Ashley. Stop worrying."

Cam checked his watch. "Your intended bride is looking this way. I think you're on."

Devon glanced over to where Ashley stood surrounded by friends and relatives. He could never sort out who was who because there were so many. She smiled and waved and then motioned him over.

He handed Cam his wineglass and made his way through the throng of people until he reached Ashley.

She sparkled tonight. She wore a radiant smile that seemed to captivate the room. But then she always drew people. She'd talk to anyone at all about anything at all.

As soon as he approached, she all but pounced on him, took his hand and dragged him into her circle. He smiled at each of the women in turn, but their names and faces kind of blended. After a moment he bent to murmur in Ashley's ear. "It's time, don't you think?"

She all but quivered in excitement. Her eyes lit up and she smiled as she squeezed his hand.

"Excuse us, ladies," he said smoothly as he drew Ashley away and back in Cam's direction. There wasn't anyone standing around Cam. Cam had that effect on people. It was the perfect place to call for attention and announce their engagement.

"Hi, Cam," Ashley sang out as they walked up to his friend. She let go of Devon's hand and threw her arms around

Cam's neck. Cam grinned and shook his head as he attempted to extricate himself from her embrace.

"Hello, Ash," he said before dropping an affectionate kiss on her cheek. "Come stand by me while Devon makes a fool of himself."

Devon sent a glare Cam's way before taking Ashley's hand and pulling her to his side. Laughing, Cam handed him a fresh wineglass and a spoon.

"What, are you kidding me?" Devon asked. "You want me to bang on a wineglass to get attention?"

Cam shrugged then tossed the spoon aside. Then he put his fingers to his lips and emitted a shrill whistle. "Everyone, I'd like your attention please. Devon here has an announcement for us."

"Thanks, Cam," Devon said dryly. Then he turned to face the room filled with Ashley's friends and relatives. And they were all staring at him expectantly. All wanting him to make this moment perfect for Ashley. Hell. No pressure or anything.

He cleared his throat and hoped like hell that he'd manage to get through it without sticking his foot in his mouth.

"Ashley and I invited you all here tonight to join us in celebrating a very special occasion." He glanced fondly down at Ashley and squeezed her hand. "Ashley has made me the happiest of men by consenting to marry me."

The room erupted in cheers and applause. To the right, Ashley's mom and dad stood beaming at their youngest child. William nodded approvingly at Devon while Ashley's mother wiped at her eyes as she smiled at her daughter.

"It's our wish that you'll all attend our wedding to take place four weeks from today and help us celebrate as we embark on our journey together as man and wife."

He held up his wineglass and turned again to Ashley whose entire face was lit up with a breathtaking smile. "To Ashley, who's made me the luckiest man alive."

Everyone raised their glasses and noisy cheers rang out again as everyone toasted Devon and Ashley.

"Quite an eloquent speech there," Cam murmured in Devon's ear. "One would almost think you meant every word."

Devon ignored Cam and slid an arm around Ashley as they braced for the onslaught of well-wishers pushing forward.

His head was spinning as he processed face after face. Bright smiles. Slaps on the back. Admonishments to take care of "their girl" as everyone in the family seemed to have a claim on Ashley.

She was everyone's younger sister, daughter, best friend or person in need of protection. It bewildered him and annoyed him in equal parts that everyone in Ashley's family seemed to think she was incapable of taking care of herself. Nothing in his relationship with Ashley had led him to believe this was an accurate assessment.

Yes, she was flighty. She was too trusting, definitely. She was a bit naive. He grimaced. He supposed he could understand that in a family of business sharks she was an anomaly, and perhaps they were right to worry that she'd be swallowed up.

But it didn't mean she was totally incapable of taking care of herself. It just meant she needed someone who'd look out for her best interests and occasionally protect her from herself. Someone like him.

Her hand feathered over his arm and she leaned up on tiptoe. He immediately lowered his head, realizing she wanted to tell him something.

"We can leave anytime," she whispered. "I know my family is a lot to take."

He almost laughed. Here he'd been thinking of how she needed his protection and she was busy protecting him from her overwhelming family.

"I'm fine. I want you to enjoy yourself. This is your night."

Her brow furrowed and her eyebrows pushed together as she stared up at him. "And not yours?"

"Of course it is. I only meant that you're surrounded by your family and friends and I want you to enjoy yourself."

She smiled, kissed him on the cheek and then settled back at his side as they were besieged my more congratulations.

"Ashley! Ashley!"

Devon turned to see a young woman barreling through the crowd practically dragging a man in her wake. He looked a bit harried but wore an indulgent smile. Devon stared a moment and then realized that whomever the woman was, she bore a striking resemblance to Ashley and she had every appearance of sharing many of the same personality traits. Probably one of her many cousins.

"Brooke!" Ashley cried. She put out her hands just as Brooke careened to a halt and Brooke grabbed hold, beaming from ear to ear.

"Guess what, guess what?" Brooke said breathlessly.

"Oh, don't make me guess. You know I'm horrible at it!" Ashley exclaimed.

"I'm pregnant! Paul and I are going to have a baby!"

Ashley's shriek of excitement could be heard over the entire room. Devon winced then quickly glanced around as everyone stared their way.

"Oh, my God, Brooke! I'm so excited for you! When? How far along are you?"

"Just ten weeks. I had to tell you as soon as I found out, but then you've been so busy with Devon and then I heard you guys were getting married and I didn't want to intrude—"

"You should have texted me at least," Ashley said. "Oh, Brooke, I'm so thrilled for you. I can only imagine how excited I'll be when I become pregnant. I hope our babies are close together and can be playmates!"

Ashley had grown louder and louder, her exuberance drawing the attention of the others, who cast indulgent smiles in Ashley's direction.

She was animated and talking a mile a minute, throwing her hands this way and that, and nearly crashed into a passing waiter. Only Devon's and Cam's quick lunge for the tray of drinks prevented complete disaster. Ashley continued, oblivious to the chaos around her.

Then she impulsively hugged Brooke again. For the third time. Then she hugged Paul. Then she hugged Brooke again, the entire time wringing her hands in excitement.

Cam chuckled and shook his head. "You've got quite the chore on your hands, Dev. Keeping up with her is going to wear your stick-in-the-mud ass out."

"Don't you have somewhere else to be and someone else to torture?" Devon muttered.

Cam glanced Ashley's way once more and Devon swore he saw genuine affection in his friend's eyes.

"She's cute," Cam said as he put his wineglass aside.

"Cute?"

Cam shifted uncomfortably. "She's sweet, okay? She seems… genuine and you can't ask for more than that."

Devon stared agape at his friend. "You like her."

Cam scowled darkly.

Devon laughed. "You like her. You, who doesn't like anyone, actually like her."

"She's nice," Cam muttered.

"But you don't think I should marry her," Devon prompted.

"Shh, she's going to hear you," Cam hissed.

But Ashley had already drifted away from Devon and was solidly ensconced in a squeal-fest with Brooke as others had heard the news and had descended. She wasn't going to hear an earthquake if a fault suddenly opened up under the building and sucked everyone in.

"If you think she's so cute and nice, why the big speech

about not being a martyr and getting married, et cetera?" Devon persisted.

Cam sighed. "Look, I just hate to see her get hurt and that's what's going to happen if you aren't straight with her. Women have a way of knowing when men aren't that into them."

"Who the hell says I'm not into her?"

Cam arched an eyebrow. "Are you saying you are? Because you don't act like a man who's into his future bride."

Devon frowned and looked around, making sure they weren't overheard. By anyone. Least of all Ashley's overprotective family. "What do you mean by that? You, Rafe and Ryan know the real circumstances of my relationship with Ashley but no one else does. I've given no one reason to suspect that I'm marrying her for any other reason than I want to."

Once again Cam shrugged. "Maybe you're right. Maybe because I know the real story it's easier for me to see that you aren't as excited as your lovely bride to be is over your impending nuptials."

"Damn it," Devon swore. "Now you're going to have me paranoid that I'm broadcasting disinterest."

"Look, forget I said anything. I'm sure it'll be fine. It's none of my business anyway. She just seems like a sweet girl and I hate to see her get hurt."

"I'm not going to hurt her," Devon gritted out. "I'm going to marry her and I'm damn sure going to take care of her."

"And you're being summoned again," Cam said, nodding in Ashley's direction. "I'm going to take off. I'll walk with you over to Ashley so I can offer my congratulations again and say good night."

Devon started in Ashley's direction then listened attentively while she introduced him to one of her cousins—one of the many in attendance—and then waited while Cam said his goodbyes and kissed her on both cheeks.

But the entire time, his mind was racing as he processed

his conversation with Cam. Was he coming across as someone who was less than enthused about his upcoming marriage? The very last thing he needed to do was drop the ball when everything was so close to being in his grasp. Finally.

He'd worked too damn hard and long to allow any slips now. If he had to wed Satan himself to seal this deal, he'd don the fire retardant suit and pucker up.

Five

No matter how many nights she'd already spent in Devon's apartment, she still got butterflies when she entered his bedroom to get ready for bed. Granted she'd only been here a week and it was still a little uncomfortable and awkward because she still didn't feel any sense of ownership when it came to his home.

She was pulling on her satin nightgown when Devon's chuckle broke the silence in the room. She turned quickly, her brow furrowed as he regarded her in amusement.

"What's so funny?"

"You. Every night you spend so much time putting on that lovely nightgown only for me to promptly take it off you when you come to bed. By now one would think you wouldn't bother."

She flushed. "It seems…presumptuous…to think you want…I mean to assume you'd want…"

"Sex?" he finished for her.

She nodded, her cheeks flaming.

He grinned and pulled her toward the bed. "I think it's a safe presumption that I'll always want sex with you. Feel free to assume all you want. I assure you…" He bent and kissed her lingeringly. "That I'll never ever…" He slid his mouth down her jaw to her neck and nibbled at her ear. "*Not* want…" He licked the pulse point at her neck, and her knees buckled. "To have sex with you. Unless I'm in a body cast and even then I'll be thinking about it."

Her nose crinkled and she shook with silent laughter. "It's true then. That sex is all a man ever thinks about?"

"We occasionally think about food."

She laughed aloud this time. "My mother is scandalized that I've practically moved in with you."

"Not practically," he said as he slid one strap over her shoulder. "You *have* moved in with me."

She shrugged. "Well she was aghast. My father told her to stop being such a worrywart, that you and I were getting married and it was only natural that we'd want time together before the big day to see if we were compatible. Eric, on the other hand, seemed pretty ticked. He thinks Daddy's nuts to *allow* me to move in with a man who's boned half the city—his words, not mine."

Devon straightened his stance and stared at her with an open mouth. "Do you *always* do that?"

She sent him a perplexed frown. "Do what?"

He shook his head. "Blurt out whatever comes to mind."

Her frown grew deeper. "Well, I guess. I mean I haven't really thought about it. It *is* what he said. I mean I didn't really pay any attention to him. He's just really protective of me and he always gets snarly when a guy starts paying attention to me."

"I hardly think me asking you to marry me can be compared to some random guy paying attention to you," he drawled.

"Well, but I'm living with you now so he obviously knows

we're having sex and he doesn't like to imagine his little sister having sex. With anyone."

Devon shuddered. "Who would?"

She grinned. "My point is, he's just being Eric and he had to get his two cents in."

"For the record, I have not *boned* half the city."

She wrapped her arms around his neck and pulled him down to kiss her. "As long as I'm the only one you'll...well, you know, in the future? I don't really care about the past."

"The future? Oh, yeah. And the present. Like right now."

She shivered as he lowered her to the bed. For having been a virgin a mere week ago, her education was no longer sorely lacking. Every night he'd taken her to places she'd only halfway imagined, and others she hadn't even known existed.

If this was a precursor to how life with him was going to be, she was going to be one very happy woman.

"Joining our meeting via video conference call this morning are Ryan Beardsley and Rafael de Luca," Devon said as his two friends' faces flashed up on the monitor on the wall. "Ryan is on location at our site build on St. Angelo Island, where our flagship resort is in its first stage of development. When completed, this resort will be the standard for every new Copeland property. Good morning, Ryan. Perhaps you could give us a progress report on the construction."

Devon tuned out Ryan and glanced over at Cam, who was slouched in a chair. Devon knew well the progress on construction. He got daily and sometimes hourly reports. Though Ryan was on site, his focus was on his very pregnant wife, who could deliver at any moment. To that end, Devon kept in contact with the foreman so that any issues that arose could be swiftly dealt with.

Cam hadn't dressed for the occasion. He'd never quite bought in to the idea that image is everything in the business world. But then he didn't really care what others thought or didn't think. It was easier for Cam, though. He'd been born to this world, while Devon had to claw and dig his way in, one torn fingernail at a time.

Cam looked like a man who could be heading to the beach for the day or at the very least planning to spend the day kicked back with a beer in one hand and a cigar in the other. But then Cam didn't drink or smoke. The man had no vices. He was disgustingly perfect in his imperfection.

Members of Tricorp's staff listened attentively to Ryan's report. Jotted down appropriate notes. The secretary took detailed minutes. There was an air of expectancy in the room. Everyone knew it was a matter of time before the big merger was announced.

Devon thought it kinder to wait. Maybe he was getting old and soft. Maybe he didn't even deserve to be on the verge of the biggest coup of his career. Because at the very moment when he stood to gain everything he'd ever wanted, he'd actually gone to William Copeland and suggested that they postpone the announcement for six months. He thought it would be kinder to Ashley if she were to think that business had nothing to do with their marriage and that the merger came after. William wouldn't have it, however. He insisted that things proceed as planned.

He thought Devon worried too much about Ashley's potential reaction. She loved him, wasn't that enough? It had made Devon cringe that apparently the whole world knew she was madly in love with her husband to be.

Besides, William pointed out that as disinterested in the family business as Ashley was, the chances of her actually putting it all together were slim. William's advice to Devon? Keep her busy and happy.

Suddenly in the midst of Ryan's report, a sound jangled over the room. There was a series of starts as his employees looked down and then around. Devon frowned. What the hell was it? It sounded like a ring tone, but it wasn't one he'd ever heard before.

Then slowly everyone's gaze turned to him and it was then he realized it was his phone going off in his pocket.

"What the hell?" he muttered.

Cam snickered.

Devon yanked his phone out of his pocket to see Ashley's name on the LCD. He nearly groaned aloud.

"Excuse me a moment," he said as he rose. "I'll take this outside."

He hurried out the door, irritated by Cam's look of amusement. He knew damn well who was calling Devon.

As soon as he was outside the conference room he punched the answer button and brought the phone to his ear. "Carter," he said tersely.

Ashley wasn't even remotely put off by his greeting. Or lack of one.

"Oh, hi, Dev! How's your day going?"

"Uh, it's good. Look, was there something you needed? I'm kind of in the middle of something here."

"Oh, nothing important," she said cheerfully. "I just wanted to call and tell you I love you."

An uncomfortable knot formed in his stomach. What was he supposed to say to that? He cleared his throat. "Ash, did you change the ring tone on my phone?"

"Oh, yeah. I did. I downloaded one so you'd know when I'm calling. Neat, huh?"

Devon closed his eyes. The cheerful cascade of noise that sounded like a cross between Tinker Bell sneezing fairy dust and a waltz at some damn princess ball would make him the laughingstock of the office in short order. Not to mention that Cam would never, ever let him live this down.

"Neat," he lamely agreed. "Look, I'll see you tonight, okay? We still on for dinner at nine?"

"Yes, that's perfect. I'm at the shelter until eight so if it's okay I'll just meet you at the restaurant."

He frowned. "Do you have a ride?"

"I'll get a cab."

He shook his head. "I'll send a car for you. Stay put at the shelter until it arrives. I'll arrange it for eight."

She sighed but didn't argue further. "Have a good day, Dev. Can't wait until tonight!"

"Thanks. You, too," Devon said but she'd already hung up.

He stared at his phone for a long moment and then punched a series of buttons. How did you even change the ring tone? He'd never designated a special ring tone for a person. His phone rang, the contact showed up, and if he wanted to answer he did. If he didn't, he let it go to voice mail. No way he wanted sparkly Tinker Bell music to play every time Ashley called him. What if she made a regular habit of it?

To his never-ending grief, she called him every single day. It baffled him that her timing was utterly impeccable. She always managed to catch him right in the middle of a meeting or when he was with a group of people.

After the second instance, he began silencing his phone and putting it on vibrate, but on two occasions, he simply forgot and his entire meeting was treated to Tinker Bell on crack.

After two weeks, he began to get amused, indulgent looks from some. Sympathy from others. Delighted grins from the women personnel. And Cam laughed his fool head off.

Ashley simply called whenever the mood struck, and unfortunately for him, he could never be sure when she would be moved to call him. Sometimes she wanted advice on wedding details. Like flowers. How the hell did he know what the difference between a tulip and a gardenia was? And invitations. Elopement to Vegas had never looked so enticing as it did right now.

Rafael and Ryan hadn't gone through all of this for their

weddings. They'd both had exceedingly simple affairs. Devon was in hell. A wedding that was being planned by the entire Copeland clan.

He was ready to throw his cell in the Hudson.

Six

"Dev?"

Devon stuck his head out of the bathroom then proceeded toward the bed, rubbing his hair with a towel. She was laying stomach down on the bed, feet dangling in the air as her jaw rested in her palm.

There was a slight frown marring her delicate features, which told him she was thinking about something. He almost didn't want to ask because he'd quickly learned that Ashley's thoughts ran the gamut.

He sat on the edge of the bed and rubbed his hand over her back. "What's up?"

She turned slightly so she could stare up at him. "Where are we going to live? I mean after we get married. We haven't really talked about it."

"I assumed we'd live here."

Her lips turned down just a bit and her brow wrinkled. "Oh."

"That doesn't sound like a good 'oh.' Do you not like the

apartment? It's bigger than yours so I naturally thought it would accommodate us better."

She scrambled up and sat cross-legged beside him. "I do like it. This is a great apartment. It's a little manly-looking. More like a bachelor pad. It's not really appropriate for children or pets."

"Pets?" he croaked out. "Uh, Ash, I don't know about pets."

Her frown deepened, which he found distressing. Ashley rarely pouted about anything, which was good, because it was damn hard to resist her when she looked unhappy. Maybe it was because she was rarely ever anything but happy.

"I've always wanted a house in the country. A place for kids and pets to run and play. The city isn't a good place to raise a family."

"Lots of people raise families here," Devon pointed out. "You were raised here."

She shook her head. "Not always, no. We didn't move to the city until I was ten. Before that we lived on this really great farm. Or at least it was a farm before my father bought it. It was such a beautiful place to live."

The wistful note in her voice was a shot to the gut.

"It's something we can discuss when the time comes," Devon said by way of appeasement. "Right now, my focus is on making you my wife, having a week of uninterrupted time with you on our honeymoon and getting you permanently moved into my apartment."

She smiled and leaned up to brush her lips across his jaw. "I love it when you talk like that."

He raised a brow as she drew back. "Like what?"

"Like you can't wait for us to be together."

She snuggled against him and wrapped her arms around his waist. And again he was assailed by an unfamiliar nagging sensation in his chest. It wasn't comfortable. He wasn't sure he liked it even as he didn't want it to go away.

"It won't be long now," he said. And then some strange urge

to continue on and at least make a token effort to lift her spirits pushed stubbornly at him. He stroked a hand over her silky hair and pressed a kiss to the top of her head. "We can always revisit the issue of where to live later. Right now, though, I want our concentration to be on each other."

She squeezed him tighter and then pulled away as she'd done before to stare up at him, her blue eyes shining. "Can we talk about one other thing?"

"Of course."

"When you say you want our concentration to be on each other, does that mean you'd prefer to wait to start a family? We've talked casually about children. I've made it no secret that I'd love to become pregnant right away but you haven't said what you want in that regard."

A sudden picture of her swollen with his child and her radiant, beautiful smile flashed through his mind. It shocked him just how gratifying the image was. He was assailed by a surge of longing and possessiveness that baffled him.

He'd always viewed marriage, a wife and eventual children with clinical detachment. Almost as if they were components of a to do list. And maybe they had been. Right underneath his goals of business success.

Now that he was suddenly faced with all of the above, he had a hard time thinking rationally about what he wanted. It was a very damn good question.

At some point he'd stopped looking at marriage to Ashley as the chore it had begun as. He'd resigned himself to the inevitability and honestly, he could do so much worse. She was intelligent, good to her core, sweet, affectionate and tenderhearted. She'd make a perfect mother. Much better than his own had ever been. But would he make a good father?

"Dev?"

He glanced down to see her staring at him with worry in her eyes. It was instinctual to want to immediately soothe the concern away. He kissed her brow. "I was just thinking."

"If it's too soon to be having this conversation, I'm sorry. Daddy always says I get too far ahead of myself. I just can't help it. I get excited about something and I just want to reach out and grab it."

He couldn't help but smile. It was such an apt description of her. She embraced life wholeheartedly. And she didn't seem to much care if she stumbled along the way. He wondered if anything ever got her down at all. People like her were a puzzle to him. He didn't understand them. Couldn't relate to them.

He pulled her onto his lap until she was astride him. "What I think is that you'll be a perfect mother. I was just imagining you pregnant with my child and decided I quite liked the image. I also had the thought that I've never used protection, which is hugely irresponsible of me even given the fact that we both have clean histories and are safe, which makes me wonder if subconsciously I was hoping to get you pregnant all along."

She sighed and went soft, melting into his chest as she leaned toward him. "I was hoping you'd say that. I mean about wanting children. It's not that I *have* to have them right away. A small part of me realizes it would probably be better to wait but I've always wanted a large family and I don't want to be old when they're graduating high school."

"You realize we've done nothing to prevent pregnancy so far," he said in a low voice.

"Do you mind?" she asked anxiously. "I mean would you be upset if I was actually pregnant before we got married?"

He chuckled. "It would be the height of hypocrisy for me to be upset over something I could have very well prevented."

"I just want to be sure. I don't want us to have a bad start. I want everything to be…perfect."

He touched her nose and then traced a path underneath her eye and down the side of her face. "Do you suspect that you're already pregnant, Ash? Is that why you're bringing this up tonight? I don't want you to be afraid to tell me anything. I'd never be angry with you for something that is equally my responsibility, if not more so. You were an innocent when I made love to you. Birth control absolutely should have been my responsibility."

She shook her head. "No. I mean I don't know. I don't think so anyway."

He rested his forehead on hers and thought for a moment that they already acted like a married couple who were at ease in their relationship. Strangely, he trusted Ashley and felt comfortable with her. There was a sense of rightness that he couldn't deny. Maybe William Copeland had known what he was doing after all.

"Well, if you are, then fantastic. Really. I want you to tell me if you even suspect you could be. And if you aren't? We'll work on remedying that. Deal?"

She grinned and a delicate blush stained her soft cheeks. "Deal."

"Now what do you say we go to bed so you can have your evil way with me?"

Her cheeks grew even redder and he smiled at the shy way she ducked her head.

He leaned in to nibble at her ear and then he whispered so the words blew gently over her skin. "I'll do my very best to make you pregnant."

To his surprise, she shoved him forward. He landed on his back on the mattress with her looming over him, a mischievous grin dimpling her cheeks. Then her expression grew more serious and her eyes darkened. "I love you so much, Devon. I'm the luckiest woman on earth. I can't wait until we're married and I'm officially yours."

As she lowered her mouth to his, he was gripped by the feeling that she was completely and utterly wrong. It wasn't she who was the lucky one.

Seven

"Ashley, if you don't sit still we're never going to get your hair and makeup right," Pippa said in exasperation.

"I still think she should have just called in a stylist," Sylvia said as she eyed the progress Tabitha was making on Ashley's hair.

"Tabitha *is* a stylist, silly," Ashley said. "She's the best and who doesn't want the best on their wedding day? And who knows more about makeup than Carly?"

Pippa snorted. "That's so true. I'm convinced cosmetic companies should just pay her to endorse their products."

"Close your eyes, Ash," Carly said. "Time for mascara. Just a bit, though. Don't want you looking clumpy on the big day."

Ashley frowned. "Definitely not clumpy."

"Darling, are you almost done?" Ashley's mother sang out from the doorway. "You're on in ten minutes."

"Ten minutes?" Tabitha shrieked. "No way. Can you stall them, Mrs. C.?"

"I'm not going to be late to my own wedding," Ashley said

firmly. "Just hurry faster, Tab. My hair will be fine. Just put the veil over the knot."

"Just put the veil over the knot," Tabitha grumbled. "As if it's that easy."

Sylvia rolled her eyes, pushed between Tabitha and Ashley and quickly affixed the veil to the elegant chignon. "There, Ashley. You look beautiful."

"Lip gloss and we're done," Carly announced. "Make a kissy face."

Ashley smacked her lips and a moment later, Carly pulled away to allow Ashley to see herself in the mirror.

"Oh, you guys," she whispered.

Her best friends beamed back at her in the mirror.

"You look beautiful," Pippa said, her eyes bright with tears. "The most beautiful bride I've ever seen."

"Absolutely you do," Tabitha said.

The four women crowded in to hug her.

"Girls, time for you to go. Your escorts are waiting. We don't want to make the bride late," Ashley's mother called.

Her friends scrambled toward the door, bouquets in hand.

"Your father is coming to get you now," her mother said as she walked over. She paused when she got to Ashley and then smiled, tears glittering in her eyes. "My baby, all grown up. You look so beautiful. I'm so proud of you."

"Don't make me cry, Mom. You know I have no willpower."

Her mom laughed and reached for her hands. She squeezed them and then helped her to her feet.

"Let me fix your gown. Your father will be pacing outside the door. You know how he hates to be late for anything."

She fussed with Ashley's dress and then there was a knock on the dressing room door.

"That will be him now. Are you ready, darling?"

Sudden nerves gripped Ashley and her palms went sweaty. But she nodded. Oh, God, this was really it. She was about to walk down the aisle and become Mrs. Devon Carter.

She threw her arms around her mom and hugged her tight. "Love you, Mom."

Her mother squeezed her back. "Love you, too, baby. Now let's go before your father wears a hole in the floor."

She went ahead of Ashley to open the door and sure enough, her father was outside checking his watch. He looked up when he heard them and his expression softened. A glimmer of emotion welled in his eyes and he held out his hand to take hers.

"I can't believe you're getting married," he said in a tight voice. "It seems like only yesterday you were learning to walk and talk. You look beautiful, Ash. Devon is a lucky man."

She leaned up to kiss his wrinkled cheek. "Thank you, Daddy. You look pretty spiffy yourself."

The wedding coordinator hurried up to them and motioned with rapid flying hands. She shooed them toward the entrance to the aisle and then spent a few seconds arranging the train of her dress.

Ashley's mom was escorted down the aisle and seated, which only left Ashley to be walked down the aisle with her father.

The music began, the doors swung open and every eye in the church turned to watch as Ashley took her first step.

Her bouquet shook in her hands and she prayed her knees would hold up. The dress suddenly seemed to weigh a ton and despite the cold outside, the church felt like a sauna.

But then she caught sight of Tabitha, Carly, Sylvia and Pippa all standing at the front of the church, their smiles wide and encouraging. Pippa winked and held a thumbs-up then pointed toward Devon and made a motion like she was fanning herself.

And finally her gaze locked on to Devon and she forgot about everyone else. Forgot about her nervousness, her sudden doubt. Nothing but the fact that he awaited her at the front of the church and that from now on, she'd belong to him.

It gave her a warm, mushy feeling from head to toe.

And then her dad was handing her over to Devon. Devon

smiled reassuringly down at her as they took the step toward the priest and the ceremony began.

It pained her to later admit that she didn't remember most of the ceremony. What she did remember was Devon's eyes and the warmth that enveloped her standing next to him as she pledged her love, loyalty and devotion. And the kiss he gave her after they were pronounced husband and wife scorched her to her toes.

Suddenly they were walking back down the aisle, this time together, as a married couple. They ducked into an alcove to await the others and Devon pulled her close into his side.

"You look absolutely stunning."

He kissed her again. This time slower. More intense. Long and lingering. He took his time exploring her mouth, and when he pulled away, she swayed and caught his arm to steady herself.

Around her, the noise of well-wishers grew and she realized that guests were coming out of the church.

"Darling, they need you back inside the church for pictures," her mother called as she hurried towards Ashley and Devon. "All your attendants are already gathered. The others are going ahead to the reception. The car is waiting to take you and Devon after you're finished with all the photos."

Devon looked less than happy at the idea of posing for so many photographs but he gave a resigned sigh and took Ashley's hand to lead her back into the sanctuary.

"It'll be over soon," she whispered. "Then we can be off on our honeymoon."

He smiled down at her and squeezed her hand. "It's the only thing making the next few hours bearable for me. The idea of you and me locked in a hotel suite for days."

She flushed but shivered in delight at the images his words invoked. She too couldn't wait for them to be alone.

But at the same time, this was her day and she was going to enjoy every single moment of it. She smiled as she was swarmed by her friends. She was surrounded by countless cousins, her uncles and aunts, her parents, her brother, distant relatives, friends.

It was truly the happiest day of her life.

Devon collected a glass of wine while Ashley's brother took his turn on the dance floor with her. Devon should probably be dancing with one of her family members but she had so many female relatives that he couldn't keep track.

Cam immediately found him and Devon whistled appreciatively to mock the formal tuxedo his friend wore.

"Only for you would I wear this getup," Cam said darkly. "I didn't wear this for Rafe's wedding and Ryan married Kelly so fast we were lucky to get a phone call saying the deed was done."

"You weren't *required* to wear one for Rafe's wedding," Devon pointed out.

Cam shrugged. "True, but then I wasn't required to wear one for yours, either. I didn't want to disappoint Ash. She thinks I look hot."

Devon shook his head. "I can't believe you've stuck around this long. Not like you to be out of your cave for such an extended period of time."

Cam made a rude noise. "I'm supposed to convey my congratulations or commiserations, whichever you need or prefer, from Rafe and Ryan. They were both sorry they couldn't make it but with wives about to drop the package at any moment, they understandably remained at home by their sides."

"You have to cut it out," Devon said. "My getting married isn't the end of the world. You didn't give Rafe and Ryan this much grief."

"Oh I did," Cam said with a grin. "I totally did. But they deserved it. They were both total douche bags."

"Like you're a shining example of chivalry, Mr. I-hate-everyone-and-women-in-particular."

Cam sobered. "Don't hate women at all. I like them too much if anything. Kind of sucks if you ask me. Besides, it's fun to give you hell. I think Ashley is perfect for a stuffy stick-in-the-mud like yourself."

"I didn't mean that, man," Devon said wearily. "I'm just on edge. I'll be glad when this is all over with. Too much stress. I've worried on a daily basis that she'd find out the truth and tell me to go to hell. The sooner we can get the hell out of here and on the plane to St. Angelo, the better I'll feel."

"For what it's worth, I wish you well," Cam said. "I think you made a huge mistake marrying someone over a business deal, but she's a sweet girl and you could certainly do worse. It's not you I worry about anyway. It's her."

"Gee, thanks," Devon said dryly. "Glad you've got my back on this one."

Cam's gaze found Ashley on the dance floor as her brother spun her around. She laughed and her smile lit up the entire room. It was clear she was having the time of her life.

"At least you won't suffer a broken heart," Cam said in a low voice. "Can you say the same for Ashley?"

"I'm not going to break her heart, damn it. Can we drop this? The last thing I need is for someone to overhear us."

"Yeah, sure. Think I'll go cut in on Ashley's brother, pay my respects to the bride before I head back to the cave you accuse me of crawling out of."

Devon watched as Cam sauntered onto the dance floor. A moment later, Eric relinquished Ashley into Cam's arms.

"You've made my little girl very happy," William Copeland said.

Devon turned around to see his father-in-law come up behind him. William smiled broadly and clapped Devon affectionately on the back. "Welcome to the family, son."

"Thank you, sir. It's an honor."

"You take Ashley and you two have a good time. Don't

worry a thing about the business. We'll have plenty of time to focus on what needs to be done when you get back."

Devon nodded. "Of course."

"Ashley's mother wanted me to tell you that the car taking you and Ashley to the airport is waiting outside. Now tradition is that you stick around, do silly stuff like cut the cake and stuff it into each other's faces, but if it were me and I'd just married one of the sweetest girls in New York City, I'd duck and make a run for it. You could be to the airport before anyone notices you're gone."

Devon smiled. "That sounds like the best plan I've heard all night. You'll cover my exit?"

William smiled back conspiratorially. "That I will, son. Go on now. Go collect your bride. Everyone here will be more than happy to eat the cake for you. No groom I ever knew gave a damn about cake anyway."

Devon laughed and then waded into the crowd to go retrieve Ashley from Cam.

Eight

The sun was sinking over the horizon when Devon carried Ashley through the doorway of their suite. As soon as he put her down, she ran to the terrace doors, flung them wide and gasped in pleasure at the burst of color splashed across the sky.

"Oh Devon, it's beautiful!"

He came up behind her, slipped his arms around her body and pulled her into his chest. He nibbled at her ear and she sighed in pleasure.

"I can't believe this is our view for the next week. Do you know how long it's been since I've been to the beach? I was a little girl."

"What?" he asked in mock horror. "You don't go to the beach?"

"I know. Terrible, isn't it? I don't know why. It's just not where our family ever went on vacation and my friends aren't really beachgoers. I just haven't made it a point to go and yet here we are and it's so fabulously gorgeous that I don't even have the words to describe it," she said breathlessly.

He chuckled. "Sounds to me like you have plenty of words. But I'm glad you like it."

She turned in his arms, allowing his hands to drop to her waist as he held her there. "How on earth did you find this place? I'd never heard of St. Angelo."

"We're constructing a resort here. We broke ground several weeks ago. Ryan and Kelly live here, remember?"

Her nose wrinkled. "Oh yes, you told me about them. I remember now. I've never met them. I've only met Cam."

"A situation I'll remedy soon. Bryony and Kelly are both very near to their due dates and so they aren't able to travel. We'll have dinner with Ryan and Kelly while we're here and I'm sure we'll have the occasion to meet Rafe and Bryony before long."

"I can't wait."

"I couldn't care less about them at the moment," Devon murmured. "I'm more interested in our wedding night."

Heat exploded in her cheeks at the same time a delicious shiver wracked her spine. "I have to get ready," she said in a low voice. "I have something special. It's a surprise."

"Mmm, what kind of surprise?"

"Umm, well, it was a gift from my girlfriends. They assured me no man alive would be able to resist me in it."

"Oh hell, remind me to thank them."

She raised an eyebrow. "You haven't seen me in it yet."

"I'll like it. I'm sure I'll like it. I'd like you in sackcloth. Whatever it is they bought you, I'm sure I'll appreciate it. Right before I peel it off your delectable body."

She all but wiggled in excitement. She was barely able to contain herself. "Okay, you wait here. Give me fifteen minutes at least. I want to look perfect. And no peeking!"

He held up his hands. "Would I do such a thing?"

Her eyes narrowed. "Promise me."

He sighed. "Okay, okay. But get moving. I'm going to go down and arrange for a very good bottle of wine and also give them our breakfast order for the morning. You have until I get back to do your thing."

She went up on tiptoe, kissed him and brushed past him into the suite. She waited just until he walked by and out of the bedroom before she hurriedly retrieved the bright pink, totally girly gift box from her suitcase.

At her lingerie shower, her girlfriends had delighted in making her eyes grow wide at all the things they'd bought her. The gifts had ranged from totally classy and elegant to absolutely outrageous and daring.

For her wedding night, she'd chosen a gown that was the perfect blend of elegant and sensual. It was sexy without being over-the-top siren material, although Ashley had no objection over the siren part. Being a seductive temptress for an evening had its merits and she was determined that she'd eventually work up the nerve to pull that one off.

She hurriedly changed and then went to survey herself in the mirror in the corner. The gown was beautiful. She felt like a princess and she liked that feeling very much. A pampered, cherished princess.

She reached for the clip holding her hair up and let the strands tumble down onto her shoulders. She fluffed it a bit, ran her fingers through the ends to straighten it and then took another step back to survey her reflection.

The bodice plunged deep between her breasts and offered just a hint of a view of the swells. If she turned just right, her nipple was almost bared. Almost, but not quite.

The skirt of the gown was sheer and it shimmered over her legs like a dream. Maybe she'd underestimated the siren quality of the lingerie. It seemed innocent enough in the box, but on her...? It took on a more seductive air and made her look less innocent and more brazen.

Not a bad look to achieve on one's wedding night.

She flashed herself an impish grin and turned away from

the mirror. Impulsively, she swirled around, outstretching her arms as she pretended to dance with an imaginary partner.

Humming lightly she twirled again, sighing dreamily as she performed the steps to the waltz she and Devon had danced at her reception. He was a good dancer. He didn't seem entirely comfortable with dancing as a rule, but he'd been more than adept at it. He moved like a dream. Commanding. Graceful with a hint of arrogance that made her all giddy inside.

She closed her eyes and whirled again. Her outstretched hand smacked against something hard and pain flashed over her knuckles at the same time a crash jolted her out of her fantasy.

Devon's laptop that had been resting on the mantel of the fireplace along with his wallet, keys and the contents of his pockets, was now lying on the floor in pieces.

She dropped to the floor, groaning her dismay. It looked as if the battery had just popped out but how could she be sure? What if she'd broken it? Who knew what all-important, irreplaceable things he had on his laptop. If he was anything like her father and brother and countless other family members, his entire life was in the damn thing.

Okay, she knew her way around computers. She may not spend her life on one, but she was capable of working one. Or determining whether or not she'd just broken her husband's.

She put the battery back in, checked for further damage and then pressed the power button, praying that it would come on. After a moment, the black screen of death remained and she let out another groan.

In frustration, she punched several buttons on the keyboard, willing something—anything—to come to life. The problem was, as soon as she began pressing the keys, the monitor blinked and she was treated to a dozen programs opening and flashing in rapid succession.

At least the damn thing worked.

She bit her lip in consternation and began closing the programs down. There were lots of Excel spreadsheets, countless charts and graphs that made her head swim. Halfway through she was struck by the fear that none of these were saved or that she was losing valuable information.

As much as she didn't want to ruin the moment, she'd be better off telling Devon what happened and let him sort out his laptop. That way tomorrow when he opened it up, there would be no nasty surprises.

She downsized the pdf that looked to be more a mammoth-sized report when her name caught her eye. She slowed down to read, her fingers pausing on the keyboard. It was an email from her father and she smiled as she saw the reference to her as his baby. But what she read next halted her in her tracks.

I've had time to consider your reservations in regard to Ashley and perhaps you were right to be concerned. I don't want you to think I discounted your intuition, but rather I want you to understand that I want her protected at all costs. Her knowing the truth of our arrangement isn't necessary even as I understand why perhaps you're uncomfortable with it. She's my only daughter and I love her dearly. The truth is, I'd rather she never know that the marriage is a condition of the merger. You are a welcome addition to this family and I trust that you'll always act in her best interests, which is why I implore you to remain silent as to our agreement.

Stunned, Ashley stared at the screen, sure that she couldn't have understood this correctly. She was jumping to conclusions, something her mother had always accused her of.

She admonished herself to remain calm even though her pulse was racing so hard that she could literally feel it jumping in her neck and in her temples.

She returned to the email, forcing the blurry words to focus.

"Ashley?"

She yanked her head up, startled as Devon suddenly loomed over her.

"It fell," she croaked out. "Off the mantel. I was afraid it was broken. The battery fell out of it. When I put it back together and started it back up, all these programs opened and I was trying to shut them all down."

He reached down to take the laptop, but she held onto it, with bloodless fingers.

He swore when he caught sight of what she was reading and he wrested the computer from her grip.

"Give it back, Devon. I want to know what it says."

He closed it with a sharp snap and tucked it underneath his arm. "There's nothing you need to see."

"Don't lie to me," she grit out. "I read most of it. Or at least the important parts. I want to know what the hell it means."

Devon stared back at her, his lips drawn in a thin line. He looked as though he'd rather be anywhere but here, doing anything but having this conversation with her. Too bad. She wasn't about to back down.

"Nothing good can come of it, Ash. Just forget it, okay?"

She gaped at him. "Forget it? You want me to just forget I saw an email from my father basically admitting he bought me a husband? Or at least manipulated you somehow into marrying me? This is my wedding night, Devon. Am I supposed to pretend I didn't see that email?"

Devon cursed and ran his hand through his hair. "Damn it, Ashley, why the hell did you open the laptop?"

"I didn't mean to! Believe me I'd give anything not to have knocked the damn thing down. But the fact is I did and now I want to know what's going on. What kind of a deal did you strike with my father? Tell me the truth or I swear I'm walking out of here right now."

"This is precisely why you're your own worst enemy at times, Ash. You're too impulsive. You don't think before you act. You just go around wading into situations and you end up getting hurt. If it enters your mind, you simply do it. That quickly. At some point you have to learn some control."

She gaped at him, openmouthed, as his frustrated, angry words bit into her. How was she the bad guy here? What the hell had she done? This wasn't her fault. She hadn't entered this marriage under false pretenses. Devon knew precisely where she stood. God knew she'd told him enough times.

His eyes flashed and he turned his back. He walked across the room to the dresser and slapped the laptop down on it. For a long moment, he stood there, not facing her, silent. Tension rose sharp and so thick it was uncomfortable. Fear struck a deep chord within her because she realized that she was about to learn something truly terrible about her life. Her fate. Her marriage.

"Devon?" she whispered.

She thought back on their relationship. The whirlwind courtship. Suddenly the blinders were off and she began to analyze every date. Everything he'd said to her. How much of it had been a lie? Was any of it true?

She didn't want to ask. She wasn't sure she could bear to know the answer to her most burning question, but she also realized she had no choice.

He turned around and his eyes were shuttered. His expression was impassive almost as if he hoped to quell any further discussion.

Suddenly the circumstances of her marriage didn't matter to her. There was only one thing she absolutely had to know. The most important thing. The one thing that would determine her future. And whether she had one with him.

"Just answer me one question," she said faintly. "Do you love me?"

Nine

Dread had a two-fisted grip around Devon's throat. He stared at Ashley's pale, stricken face and he knew his time had come. Maybe he'd always known that this moment would come. He'd never really believed that it was possible to prevent Ashley from finding out the truth and furthermore it was stupid to try to keep it from her.

Damn fool of an old man. William Copeland didn't want his precious daughter hurt and yet he'd set her up for the biggest fall of her life. Nice. And now Devon was going to look like the biggest bastard of all time.

"I care for you a great deal," he said evenly.

Anger and fear warred with one another in her eyes. His answer sounded lame even to his own ears but he couldn't bring himself to destroy her even further. Hadn't she endured enough already?

"Let's have the truth," she demanded. "Don't patronize me or pat me on the head while whispering pretty words to pacify me. It's a very simple question, Devon. Do you love me?"

His nostrils flared. "The truth isn't always a pretty thing, Ash. The truth isn't always pleasant to hear. Be careful when you ask for the truth because it can hurt far more than not knowing."

If possible she went even paler. Her eyes were stricken and all the light vanished from their depths as if someone had extinguished a flame. For a moment he thought she'd let it go, but then she squared her shoulders and said in a low, dead voice, "The truth, Dev. I want the truth. I need to hear it."

He bit out another curse and thrust his hand into his hair. "All right, Ashley, no, I don't love you. I care about you a great deal. I like and respect you. But if you want to know if I love you, then no."

She made a broken sound of pain that was like a knife right through his chest. Why couldn't he have just lied to her? Because she would have known the truth whether he admitted it or not and she'd already been deceived enough.

And maybe now they could finally go forward with complete and utter honesty and he could stop feeling like the worst sort of bastard at every turn.

She started to step backward, but she swayed precariously and flailed out one arm to catch herself on the mantel. He bolted forward, caught her shoulders and then guided her to the bed, forcing her down into a sitting position.

He took one step back and then heaved out a breath. Before he could launch into what he wanted to say, she found his gaze and he flinched at the raw vulnerability reflected in those eyes.

"What a fool I've made of myself," she whispered. "How stupid and naive. How you must have laughed."

"Damn it, Ash, I've never laughed at you. Never!"

"I loved you," she said painfully. "Thought you loved me. Thought we were getting married because you wanted me, not my father's business or whatever it was he offered you. How much did I cost you, Dev? Or should I ask how much my father offered you to marry me?"

Furious at the senseless direction this was heading, he yanked the chair out from the desk, turned it around and sat so he faced her.

"Listen to me. There's no reason we can't have an enjoyable marriage. We're compatible. We get along well together. We're good in bed. Those are three things many married couples don't have going for them."

She closed her eyes.

"Look at me, Ash. This may be painful to hear but maybe it's for the best if we get it all out in the open. You're far too emotional. You wear your feelings and your heart on your sleeve and it's only going to get you hurt. Maybe it's time for you to grow up and face the fact that life isn't a fairy tale. You're too impulsive. You dash about with no caution and no sense of self-preservation. That's only going to cause you further pain down the road."

She shook her head in utter confusion. Her eyes were cloudy and it was clear she was battling tears. "How could I possibly ever hurt as much as I do now? How can you be so...so... *cold* and calm and so matter-of-fact as if this is nothing more than a business meeting where you're discussing figures and projections and sales and a whole host of other things I don't understand?"

His gut twisted into a knot. He'd never felt so damn helpless in his life. He wished to hell it was as simple as telling her to be harder and for her not to let this destroy her, but he knew it was pointless because Ashley was one of the most tenderhearted people he knew and he was an ass to sit here and tell her to get over it.

She covered her face in her hands and he could see her throat working convulsively as she tried to keep her sobs silent. But they spilled out, harsh and brittle in the quiet.

He lifted his hand to touch her hair but left it in the air before finally pulling it back. She wouldn't welcome comfort from him, of all people. If it were any other woman, she'd have already come after his nuts and he'd deserve everything she dished out and more.

"Ash, please don't cry."

She lifted her ravaged face and pushed angrily at her hair. "Don't cry? What the hell else do you suggest I do? How could you do this? How could my father? Tell me, Devon, what was the price put on my future? What do you get out of the bargain?"

He stared at her in silence.

"Tell me, damn it! I think I deserve to know what my happiness was traded for."

"Your father wanted me to marry you as part of the merger between Tricorp Investments and Copéland Hotels," he bit out. "Happy now? Can you tell me what possible good it does for you to know that?"

"It doesn't make me happy but I damn well want to know what I've gotten myself into, or rather what my father got me into. Did I ever even have a chance? Did you study up on all the ways to worm your way into my heart?"

"Christ, no. Look, it was all real. It's not like I faked an attraction to you. It wasn't exactly a hardship to pursue you. If I hadn't wanted to marry you, no merger or deal would have persuaded me differently. I thought and still think that we'd make a solid marriage. I don't see why love has to be the be-all and end-all in this equation. Mutual respect and friendship are far more important aspects of a relationship."

"Maybe you can tell me how the hell I'm supposed to respect a man who doesn't love me and who manipulated me into a marriage based on deception. Does everyone think I'm a brainless twit who should be pathetically grateful that a man sweeps into my life and offers to take care of me? I've got news for you and my family. I hadn't married yet because it was my choice. I hadn't had sex with a man yet because I had enough respect for myself that I wasn't going to be pressured into something I wasn't ready for. It's not like I haven't had men interested in me. I'm not pathetically needy nor was I going to waste away if I wasn't married by the ripe old age of twenty-three. I was happy. I had a good life."

"Ashley, listen to me."

He leaned forward, caught her hands and stared until she quieted and returned his gaze.

"Right now you're upset and you're hurting. But don't discount the possibility that we could enjoy a comfortable, lasting marriage. Don't make a snap decision you may regret later. Take some time to think about it when you've calmed down. When you're not so volatile, you'll be able to look at the situation more objectively."

"Oh screw off," she snapped. "Could you be any more patronizing? 'Don't be so high-strung, Ashley. Don't be so stupid and naive. Don't expect ridiculous things like love and affection in a marriage. How perfectly absurd would that be?'"

"I don't think we should have this conversation any longer," he said tightly. "Not until you've had time to calm down and think about what you're saying." He stood abruptly and she looked hastily away but not before he saw the silver trail of her tears streaking down her cheeks.

He wanted more than anything to pull her into his arms and let her cry on his shoulder. He wanted to comfort her, hold her, soothe her fears and tell her it would be all right. But how could he when he was the sole reason she was devastated?

"I'm sorry, Ash," he said hoarsely. "I know you don't believe that, but I'm more sorry than you'll ever know. I would have done anything at all to spare you this pain."

"Please, just go away and leave me alone," she choked out. "I can't even look at you right now."

He hesitated a moment and then sighed in resignation. "I'll take the couch in the living area. We'll talk more in the morning."

It took every ounce of his willpower to turn around and walk out of the bedroom. His instincts screamed at him not to leave her alone. To take her in his arms and force the issue. Make her listen to him. To not relent until she agreed that their marriage could and would work if only they could set aside the emotional volatility that always seemed to accompany declarations of love.

He had only to point at his friends to know this was an inevitable truth. Their lives were emotional messes brought on by the letter *L*.

All that angst and suffering in the name of love. Rafe and Ryan had spent more time in abject misery and all because they'd been ripped to shreds by…love.

Devon grimaced and sank onto the couch in the dark living room. What a wedding night this had turned out to be. Maybe he'd always known that it was inevitable that she learn the truth. How could she not? But he'd hoped they'd have a lot more mileage behind them. Then she could see that their marriage wasn't defined by love or emotion, volatility or vulnerability.

Friendship, companionship, trust, respect.

Those were all things he was on board with.

Love? Not so much. It was a messy, raw emotion he had no desire to embroil himself with.

Ten

Ashley sat on the private veranda and stared over the ocean as the sun began its hesitant rise. She felt empty. Rung out. She felt stupid and so horribly naive that she cringed. It still baffled her that a life she'd thought was so perfect just hours before was a complete facade.

All night she'd sat huddled in an uncomfortable chair trying to come to grips with the fact that she'd been lied to at every turn. She'd been used and manipulated, not just by Devon, but by her own father. And all over a business deal.

She couldn't wrap her head around it.

Why? Why had it been so important for Devon to marry her? Was her father so unconvinced of Ashley's ability to manage her own life that he'd all but hired a man to be her husband? She winced at the thought, but it was appropriate. At the very least, she'd been used as a bargaining chip.

She rubbed at eyes that felt full of sand. She'd cried all that she was going to allow herself to cry. She be damned if she shed another single tear over her husband.

A dry laugh escaped her. Her husband. What was she going to do about her marriage? Her complete and utter farce of a marriage.

She closed her eyes against the humiliation of it all. What a fool she'd made of herself over the last month. She wanted to die from it.

Had he laughed at her the entire time? Had he joked with his friends about what a gullible idiot she was? She didn't like to imagine he could be so cruel, but the man she'd faced down the night before and demanded the truth from had been brutally honest. At her insistence, but crushingly forthright all the same.

"It's time you had the cold hard truth, Ashley," she whispered. She'd been living a fantasy.

She rubbed at her temples, willing the vicious ache to go away. But the pain in her head was nothing compared to the unbearable ache in her heart.

Should she leave him? Should she ask for a divorce? They could have the shortest marriage on record. She could go back home. Chalk it up to a lesson learned the hard way. It was doubtful at this point that her father would pull the plug on the deal because Devon had lived up to his end of the bargain. It wasn't Devon who was unhappy with the result. It was her. Everyone had evidently thought she was the very last person who should be consulted about her life.

But the idea of divorcing Devon held as little appeal as living in the cold, sterile state her marriage now existed in. She deeply loved him and love wasn't something you could switch off at will. She was hurt beyond belief. She was angry and she felt horribly betrayed. But she still loved him and she still wished that they could go back to the way things had been before she'd found out the damnable truth.

It was true what they said about ignorance being bliss. She'd give anything at all to go back to being that innocent little girl who still believed in happily ever after with Prince Charming.

For just a little while Devon had been that prince. He'd been perfect. She'd built him into something he wasn't, and that wasn't entirely his fault. He couldn't be blamed for her utter stupidity.

No, she didn't want a divorce. But neither did she want to live a life with a man who didn't love her.

She thought back to all the things he'd said to her the night before. His criticisms had stung. They'd stunned her. She'd never imagined that he'd thought of her in such a negative way. But maybe he was right.

Maybe she was too impulsive, too flighty, too exuberant. Perhaps she should be more controlled, more guarded, show more of a knack for self-preservation.

It was evident that he didn't want the person she was. It was evident he didn't love flighty, impulsive, tender-hearted, animal-loving Ashley Copeland, who called him at work just to say she loved him.

If he didn't want or love that person, then the only two options left to her were to walk away and get a divorce or to *become* someone he could love.

Could she make him fall in love with her? Her family always worried that she was too trusting. Too naive. Too everything. Apparently they were right.

The only person who didn't seem to think anything was wrong with who Ashley Copeland was, was Ashley herself. And it was becoming increasingly clearer that her judgment stank.

It was time for one hell of a makeover.

But the idea didn't excite her. It didn't infuse enthusiasm into her flagging spirits. It was a bleak thought and she dimly wondered if Devon was worth such an effort.

Would his love be enough, provided she could even make him fall in love with her?

A voice in the back of her mind whispered that it was time for her to grow up. It was a voice that sounded precariously close to Devon's. He thought she should grow up. Her father evidently thought the same. Maybe they were both right.

She stiffened when she heard a sound on the terrace. She knew it was Devon but she wasn't ready to face him yet.

"Have you been out here all night?" he asked quietly.

She nodded wordlessly and continued to stare over the water.

He walked to the thick stone railing that enclosed the private viewing area, shoved his hands in his pockets and for a moment stared over the water as she was doing. Then he turned to face her and leaned back against the stone.

He looked as bad as she felt, though she had no sympathy. His hair was rumpled. He was still in the same clothes as the night before.

"Ash, don't torture yourself over this. There's no reason we can't have a perfectly good marriage, no matter the circumstances of *how* we came to be married."

He was starting to repeat his arguments from the previous night and the truth was, she couldn't stomach hearing again how she was naive and impulsive and whatever else it was he'd said when he outlined all her faults.

She bit her lip to keep the angry flood from rushing out because at this point it did her no good and she didn't have the emotional energy to spare.

She held up a hand to stop him and cursed at how it trembled. She put it back down and tucked it into her gown, blinking as she realized she was still in her sexy, lacy lingerie that she'd so painstakingly picked out for her wedding night.

Unbidden tears welled again in her eyes as she realized just what a disaster her wedding night had been. What should have been the most special night of her entire life would forever be a black hole in her past no matter what happened in the future.

"I agree," she said before he could launch into another list of her shortcomings.

He promptly shut his mouth and then stared at her, his brows drawn together in confusion. "You do?"

She nodded again because the words seemed to stick in her throat. Almost as if they were rebelling. It took her a few moments to force out what she wanted to say.

"You're absolutely right. I was being silly. I had unrealistic expectations and I shouldn't allow them to get in the way of marriage."

He winced but remained quiet.

"I am agreeable to at least a period of time in which we see how things progress."

He frowned at that but she looked up with dead eyes. "Be glad I'm not on a plane home with an appointment to see a divorce lawyer."

He pushed out a breath and then slowly nodded. "All right. How long do you think this test period will last?"

She shrugged. "How would I know? I can't exactly put a time frame on when I can give up all hope of having a happy marriage."

"Ash."

The low growl in which he said her name only served to make her angrier. She curled her fingers into tight balls, determined not to give in to the urge to scream at him. She was determined to get through this, no matter how excruciating it was.

"I'm not trying to punish you, Devon. I'm trying to get through this without losing what little pride I have left."

He went pale and pain flickered in his eyes. And shame. Though that hadn't been her intention, either. She wasn't trying to make digs at him because that wouldn't make this go away. It wouldn't give her back her happiness. It would only make her more miserable than she already was.

"You seem to think we can have an enjoyable marriage. I personally find no joy in being married to a man who doesn't love me, but I'm willing to try. You're probably right in that I shouldn't allow something so silly as love to enter the equation."

"Damn it, I care a lot for you—"

"Please," she bit out, halting his words in midsentence. "Just don't. Don't try to make it better by offering me platitudes. It was hard to hear your assessment of my faults. Does anyone ever like to hear that about themselves? But I'm willing to work on not being so impulsive and exuberant or whatever else it was that you mentioned. I'll try to be the best wife I can be and not disappoint you."

He bit out a sharp curse but she ignored him and plunged ahead before she lost all her courage and fled.

"I just have one thing to ask in return," she whispered.

She was trying valiantly not to break down again. She'd already made such an idiot of herself in front of him. She was forever making a total cake of herself with him.

His lips were thin. His eyes were dark with raw emotion. At least he wasn't totally unaffected by her distress.

"I find the situation I'm in immensely humiliating. I'll make every effort to be a wife you'll be proud of. All I ask is that you please not embarrass me in front of my family by making our issues known to anyone. What I'm asking you to do is pretend. At least with them."

"God, Ash. You act as though I despise you. I'd never embarrass you."

"I just don't want them to know you don't love me," she choked out. "If you could just act like—like a real husband in front of them. You don't have to go overboard. Just don't treat me with indifference now that you don't have to pretend in order to get me to marry you anymore."

And then another thought occurred to her that very nearly had her leaning over to empty the contents of her stomach.

"Are you all right?" Devon asked sharply. Then he swore. "Of course you aren't all right. You look as if you're going to be ill."

"Is there someone else?" she croaked out. "I mean did you ever plan to be faithful? I won't stay married to you if you're going to sleep around or if you have a mistress on tap somewhere."

This time the curses were more colorful and they didn't stop for several long seconds. He closed the distance between them, knelt down in front of the lounger she was curled up in and grasped her shoulders.

"Stop it, Ashley. You're torturing yourself needlessly. There is no other woman. There won't be another woman. I take my marriage vows very seriously. I don't have a mistress. There's been no other woman since well before you entered the picture. I have no desire to sleep around. I want *you*."

Her shoulders sagged in relief and she leaned away from him so that his hands slipped from her arms.

"Damn it, I wanted to tell you the truth from the very beginning but your father wouldn't hear of it. My mistake. I should have told you anyway. But it doesn't change anything. I still want to be married to you. If I found the idea so abhorrent, I'd simply wait until the deal was done and begin divorce proceedings. There wouldn't be a damn thing your father could do at that point."

She closed her eyes wearily and rubbed at her head. The sun's steady creep over the horizon was casting more light onto the terrace and each ray speared her eyeballs like a flaming pitchfork.

"Do you have one of your headaches?" he asked, his voice full of concern. "Did you bring your medicine?"

She opened her eyes again, wincing as she tried to refocus. "I want to go home."

Devon's expression darkened. "Don't be unreasonable. What you need is to take your medicine and get some sleep. You'll feel better once you rest and eat something."

"I won't stay here and pretend. It's pointless. You even brought me to the island where you're building a resort, I'm sure so you could keep up with the progress. So don't tell me I'm being unreasonable for wanting to dispense with the fairy-tale honeymoon. You and I both know at this point it's a joke and we'll just spend all week staring awkwardly at each other or you'll just spend most of the time at the job site."

His jaw ticked and he stood again, turning briefly away. Then he turned back, irritation evident in his gaze. "You wanted me to pretend in front of your family. Why can't you pretend now?"

"Because I'm miserable and it's going to take me a little time to get over this," she snapped. "Look, we can say I wasn't feeling well. Or you can make up some business emergency. It's not as if anyone in my capitalistic family would even lift an eyebrow at the idea of business coming first. Right now my head hurts so damn bad, we wouldn't even be lying."

Some of the anger left Devon's gaze. "Let me get you some medication for your headache. Then I want you to get some rest. If..." He sighed. "If you still want to leave when you wake up, I'll arrange our flight back to New York."

Eleven

She slept because the pill Devon gave her would allow her to do no less. She rarely resorted to taking the medication prescribed for her migraines for the reason that it made her insensible.

When she awoke, she was in bed by herself and it was nearly dusk. Her headache still hung on with tenacious claws and when she moved too suddenly to try to sit up, nausea welled in her stomach. Her head pounded and she put a hand to her forehead, sucking air through her nostrils to control the sudden wash of weakness.

The room was blanketed in darkness, the drapes drawn and no lights had been left on. Devon had made sure she had been left in comfort, only a sheet covering her and the air-conditioning turned down so it was nearly frigid in the room.

Before, his consideration would have been endearing. Now, she could only assume he was operating out of guilt.

She pushed herself from the bed and sat on the edge for a moment, holding her head while she got her bearings. After a moment, she got to her feet and wobbled unsteadily toward the luggage stand, where her still-packed suitcase lay open.

She ripped off the silky gown she'd so excitedly donned the night before and tossed it in the nearby garbage can. If she never saw it again, it would be too soon.

She dug through the suitcase, bypassing the chic outfits, the swimwear and the other sexy nightwear she'd purchased, and pulled out a faded pair of jeans and a T-shirt. She briefly contemplated shoes, but the idea had formed in her head to take a long walk on the beach. Maybe it would clear her head or at least stop the vile aching. For that, she wouldn't need shoes.

Having no idea where Devon was, or if he was even still in the suite, she opted to leave through the sliding glass doors to the veranda. The breeze lifted her hair as soon as she walked outside the room and she inhaled deeply as she took the steps leading down to the beach.

The night was warm and the wind coming off the water was comfortable, but she was cold to her bones and she shivered as her feet dug into the sand.

It was a perfect, glorious night. The sky was lit up like a million fireflies had taken wing and danced over the inky black canvas. In the distance the moon was just rising over the water and it shimmered like a splash of silver.

Drawn to the mesmerizing sight, she ventured closer to the water, hugging her arms around her waist as the incoming waves lapped precariously close to her toes.

At one point, she stopped and allowed the water to caress her feet and surround her ankles. There she stood, staring over the expanse of the ocean, stargazing like a dreamer. It would take a million wishes to fix the mess she was currently in. And maybe that was what had gotten her into this situation in the first place.

Stupid dreams. Stupid idealism. She'd been a fool to wait for the perfect guy to give her virginity to. She'd always been somewhat smug and a little holier-than-thou with her friends who'd given it up long ago. But they at least had gone into the situation with their eyes wide open. They hadn't confused sex for love. They weren't the ones on their honeymoon with the migraine from hell and a husband who didn't love them.

They were looking pretty damn smart for shopping around and Ashley was looking like a moron.

She pulled out her cell phone and stared down at her contacts list. She could use the comfort of a good friend right now but she wavered on whether to send a text. She was already humiliated enough. Could she bear to tell her friends or even one friend the truth about her marriage? Or would she go back home, live a lie and hope that Devon would pretend as agreed.

Could she ever make him love her?

She lowered the hand holding the phone and then she shoved it back into her pocket. What could she say anyway in the limited number of characters allowed by a text message? Or maybe she should just tweet everyone.

Marriage fail. Honeymoon fail.

That would get the message across with plenty of characters left over.

She shoved her hands into her pockets, closed her eyes and wished for just one minute that she could go back. That she would have asked more questions. That she would have picked up on the fact he'd never said he loved her even when Ashley made it a practice to tell him every day.

She'd just assumed he was a typical guy. Devon was reserved. He was somewhat forbidding. But she'd been wildly attracted to those qualities. Thought they were sexy. She'd been convinced that he quietly adored her and that his actions spoke louder than words.

She'd never considered even once that his actions were practiced, fake and manipulative.

Another shiver overtook her and she clamped her teeth together until pain shot through her head.

"Enough," she said.

She had beat herself up for the last twenty-four hours, but it was Devon who was the jackass here. Not her. She'd done nothing wrong. Naiveté wasn't a crime. Loving someone wasn't a crime. She wouldn't apologize for offering her love, trust and commitment to a man who didn't deserve any of it.

He was wrong. She wasn't.

The only thing she could control from here on out was what she did with the truth. It was no longer about what Devon wanted. If he could be a selfish jerk-wad, she could at least focus on what she wanted from this fiasco.

Then she laughed because what she wanted was the jerk-wad to love her. That might make her pathetic.

No, she couldn't text Sylvia or Carly or Tabitha. Definitely not Pippa. Pippa would have her in front of a lawyer in a matter of hours and then she'd likely take out a hit on Devon.

Plus her friends would tell her she was being stupid for wanting to stay in the marriage. And she may well be an idiot, but she didn't want people telling her that. She'd already made one mistake. It wouldn't be the first or last and well, if it didn't work out, at least then she could cite incompatibility and she wouldn't have to tell everyone that the marriage had fallen apart before it had ever gotten off the ground.

She had just enough of an ego to want to save face. Who could blame her?

Feeling only marginally better about taking control over a perfectly out-of-control situation, she turned to retrace her steps. She was hungry but the thought of food made her faintly nauseous and her head was hurting so badly she wasn't sure she could keep anything down anyway.

She was still a good distance from the steps leading to her and Devon's suite when she saw him striding toward her on the sand.

Even now after so much time to think and decide how she wanted to proceed, she wasn't prepared to face him. How could she just go on after finding out he was nothing like the man she'd thought she'd married? It was as if they were strangers. Intimate strangers who would now live together and pretend a loving existence to outsiders.

There weren't manuals for this. Certainly no one had ever given her advice on such a matter. She wasn't good at artifice. She hated lying. But it was what she'd asked him to do. It was what she herself had just decided to do with her friends and family. To the world.

"Where the hell have you been?" Devon demanded as he approached. "I was worried sick. I went in to check on you and you were gone."

Before she could answer, he put his hand around her elbow and pulled her toward the glow cast from the torches that lined the beach.

She flinched away from the burst of light and he muttered something under his breath.

"Your headache isn't any better, is it?"

She slowly shook her head.

"Damn it, Ash, why didn't you come to me? Or take another pill. You should be in bed. For that matter you've eaten nothing in twenty-four hours. You're as pale as death and your eyes are glazed with pain."

She braced herself as he reached for her again, but his touch was in direct contrast to the tone of his voice. He was infinitely gentle as he pulled her against his side and began leading her back to the suite.

Unable to resist the urge, she laid her head on his shoulder and closed her eyes, trusting him to at least get her safely up the steps. His hold tightened around her and then to her shock, he simply swung her into his arms and began carrying her back.

"Put your head on my shoulder," he said gruffly.

Relaxing against him, she did as he directed and for a few moments, basked in the tenderness of his hold.

Pretending was nice.

He carried her back into the suite, into the still-darkened bedroom, and carefully laid her on the bed.

"Would you be more comfortable out of your jeans?" he asked. But even as he asked, he was unfastening her fly and pulling the zipper down.

He efficiently pulled her pants down her legs, leaving her in her panties and T-shirt. She lay there, cheek resting on the firm, cool pillow, and willed the pain to go away. All of it.

He sat on the edge of the bed and then turned, sliding his leg over the mattress and bending it so he was perched next to her.

"I'll get you another pill, but I don't think you should take it on an empty stomach. It might make you ill. But neither do you look as though you could keep down much so I'll call down for some soup. Would you like something to drink? Could you handle some juice?"

As he spoke, he smoothed his hand over her hair, stroking gently, and she had to bite her lip to keep the hot tears from slipping down her cheeks again. This wasn't going to work if she broke down every time he was nice to her or took care of her.

And it wasn't as if he was doing anything different than he'd done all along. It was one of the things that had made her think he loved her to begin with, even absent of the actual words. He'd been so...good...to her. So caring. Protective. Possessive. A guy couldn't fake all of that, could he?

"Soup sounds good," she said faintly.

He continued to stroke her hair and then his hand went still and he frowned. "Is that bothering you? I wasn't thinking. I'm sure you must be supersensitive to any touch or sound."

"It was...nice."

"I'll be right back. Let me order your soup. You need to get something in your stomach. It might help with the headache, too."

She closed her eyes as he stood and walked across the room.

He stepped outside but she could just make out the low murmur of his voice as he ordered room service. A moment later, he returned and gently laid his hand over her forehead.

"It'll be here in a few minutes. I told them to put a rush on it."

"Thank you."

He was silent for a few seconds and then he said in a voice full of resignation, "I'll make arrangements for us to fly home in the morning. Perhaps it's best if you're back in familiar surroundings. I don't want you to suffer with a headache the entire week we were supposed to be here. At least at home, you'll have your family and your friends to surround you and…make you feel better."

She nodded, her chest heavy and aching with regret. It should have been different. They should have spent the week making love. Laughing. Spending every waking moment immersed in each other.

Instead they'd go back home to a very uncertain future in a world that was suddenly unfamiliar to Ashley. Where she'd have to guard every word, every action.

It frightened her. What if she failed? What if even after she removed the annoyances he still felt nothing more for her than he did now?

Then he doesn't deserve you, the voice inside her aching head whispered in her ear.

He didn't deserve her now. The intelligent side of her knew and accepted this. But she wanted him. Wanted his love, his approval. She wanted him to be proud of her.

If that made her an even bigger moron than she'd already been, she could live with that. What she couldn't live with was just walking away without seeing if their marriage could be salvaged.

"It will be better when we get home," she whispered.

His hand stilled on her hair but he remained silent as he

seemed to contemplate her words. His expression was grim and tension radiated from his body in waves.

Then there was a distant knock and he rose once more. "That'll be the food. Just stay here. I'll wheel the cart in and we'll get you a comfortable spot made up so you can eat in bed."

He strode out of the room and Ashley lay there a moment mentally recovering from what felt like a barrage of emotional turmoil. Finally she pushed herself upward and sat cross-legged on the bed, with pillows pushed behind her back to keep her propped up.

Devon returned with the rolling table and parked it at the end of the bed. As soon as he uncovered the bowl of soup, the aroma wafted through the air and her mouth watered. On cue, her stomach protested sharply and sweat broke out on her forehead.

"You okay?" Devon asked as he positioned the tray in front of her.

His gaze was focused sharply on her face, his forehead creased with concern. She nodded and reached for the napkin and utensils with shaking hands.

When she would have slid the bowl closer, Devon gently took her hand away.

"Perhaps it would be better if I ladled the soup into a mug so you could sip at it. Less chance of spilling it that way."

She nodded her agreement and watched as he filled one of the cups on the table with the delicious-smelling broth.

"Here. Careful now, it's hot."

She brought the steaming mug to her lips and inhaled, closing her eyes as she tentatively took the first sip.

It was heaven in a coffee cup. The warmth from the soup traveled all the way down to her stomach and settled there comfortably.

"Good?" he asked as he edged his way onto the bed beside her.

"Wonderful."

He watched as she downed a significant amount of the soup and then he took her medicine bottle from the nightstand and shook out another pill.

"Here. Take this. Once you're finished you can lie down and hopefully sleep until morning. I'll wake you up in time to catch the flight. Don't worry about your things. I'll lay out something for you to wear on the plane and I'll pack everything else and have it all ready to go. All you'll have to do is get dressed and head out to the car when it's time."

Even though she was still devastated and angry, she couldn't be so much of a bitch not to recognize or acknowledge that he was taking absolute care of her.

She leaned back against the pillows, cup in hand, and glanced his way.

"Thank you," she said quietly.

A flash of pain entered his eyes. "I know you don't believe this right now, but maybe in time you will, Ash. I never meant to hurt you. I never wanted this to happen. I wouldn't have hurt you for the world."

She swallowed and brought the rim of the cup back to her lips. There wasn't much she could say to that. She did believe that he wasn't malicious. If she hadn't discovered the truth on her own, maybe he would have never told her. She was quite certain he wouldn't have. Maybe he thought he was doing her a favor by keeping it from her.

He pulled the mug away and then cupped her chin and gently turned her until she looked back at him.

"You'll see, Ash. We'll make this work."

She nodded as she lowered the mug the rest of the way down to the tray in front of her.

"I'll try, Devon. I'll try."

He leaned toward her and pressed a kiss to her forehead. "Get some rest. I'll wake you in the morning."

Twelve

The next morning was a total blur for Ashley. Devon gently woke her and after ascertaining that her headache wasn't better, he arranged a light breakfast, hovered over her while she ate and then all but dressed her and whisked her into a waiting car.

They drove to the airport and once on the plane, he settled her into her seat and gave her another pill. He propped a pillow behind her head, put a blanket over her and then made sure every single window was shut around her.

She drifted into blissful unawareness as the airplane left the island and traveled back to the cold of New York City.

When they landed, once again Devon ushered her into a waiting car, taking the blanket and pillow with them so she was comfortable in the backseat. She dozed with her head on his shoulder until they reached his apartment and then he gently shook her awake.

"We're home, Ash. Wait inside the car while I get out. I'll help you inside."

Home. She blinked as the looming building floated into her vision through the fogged window of the car. A cold rush of air blew over her as Devon stepped out. He spoke a moment with the doorman and then he reached back in to help her out.

"Careful," he cautioned as she stepped onto the curb.

He wrapped an arm around her and guided her to the door the doorman held open for them. Once inside, he didn't loosen his hold. He kept her close all the way up in the elevator until they reached his apartment. Their apartment. It was hard to keep that distinction in her mind.

Their home was already cluttered with her things. She'd moved completely in before the wedding. Devon had suggested having a cleaning lady come in which said to her that he didn't appreciate the somewhat careless way she kept her stuff. She sighed. One more thing she'd have to work on.

When they entered the bedroom, Devon pulled out one of his workout T-shirts and tossed it onto the bed. "Why don't you get out of your travel clothes and into something more comfortable. I'll wake you for dinner so you eat something."

"I'd rather just lie down on the couch," she said, reaching for the T-shirt.

His expression darkened and for a moment she couldn't imagine what she'd done to draw his disapproval. Then it struck her that he assumed she wouldn't be sleeping in his— their—bed.

It wasn't something she'd given any consideration. The thought hadn't even occurred to her. In her mind, if she was staying and making an effort to make their marriage work, she just naturally assumed they'd still sleep together.

Perhaps it wasn't something she should assume at all. She sank onto the edge of the bed, still foggy and loopy from the medication. She rubbed wearily at her eyes before focusing back on him.

"I only meant that when I have a headache, sometimes I'm more comfortable propped on the couch so I'm not lying flat.

However, it does bring up a point that I hadn't considered. I assumed that we'd continue to…" She swallowed, suddenly feeling vulnerable and extremely unsure of herself. "That is, I just thought we'd continue to sleep together. I have no idea if that's something you want."

Devon stalked over, bent down and placed his hands on either sides of her legs so that he was on eye level with her.

"You'll be in my bed every night. Whether we're having sex or not, you'll be next to me, in my arms."

"Well, okay then," she murmured.

He rose and took a step back. "Now, if you're more comfortable on the couch, change into my shirt and I'll get you pillows and a blanket for the couch."

She nodded and sat there watching him as he walked away. She glanced around the room—to all her stuff placed haphazardly here and there—and sighed. When she got rid of this headache, she'd whip the apartment into shape. She'd been away from the shelter more days than she'd ever been away before but the animals were in good hands and they'd be fine while she got the rest of her life in order.

Devon would no doubt be back to work in the morning, which meant she'd have plenty of time alone to figure out things. She wrinkled her nose. Being alone sucked. She was always surrounded by people. In her family she didn't have to look far if she wanted company. There was always someone to hang out with. And aside from her family, her circle of friends was always available even if for a gab session.

But what was she supposed to talk to them about now? How wonderful her marriage was? Her husband? The aborted honeymoon?

Her head was too fuzzy to even contemplate the intricacies of her relationships right this second. She reached for the T-shirt, shed her own clothes and crawled into Devon's shirt.

She started to leave her clothes just where they'd dropped on the floor, but she stopped to pick them up and then deposited them into the laundry basket in the bathroom. It was technically Devon's basket and he might not want her mixing her clothes with his, but she didn't have a designated place of her own yet. One more thing for the to-do list.

She trudged out to the living room to see that Devon had arranged several pillows and put out a blanket for her. As she started across the floor, Devon appeared from the kitchen. She crawled onto the couch and burrowed into all of the pillows while Devon pulled the blanket up to her shoulders. Then he perched on the edge close to her head.

"Are you feeling any better yet?"

She nodded. "Head doesn't hurt as bad. A few more hours and it should be fine. Just fuzzy from all the medication. I've never had to take three in a row like that."

He frowned as if he realized the significance of her having the worst headache of her life after their confrontation.

"Rest for a few hours then. I'll check on you in a bit and see if you're up for some dinner. I thought we'd eat in, of course. I can order anything you like or if you prefer, I can make something here."

She nodded.

"I have some calls to make. I'll let your family know we're back and why. You just concentrate on feeling better."

Her eyes widened in alarm. "What are you going to tell them?"

He frowned again. "I'm only going to tell them that you came down with a severe headache and that we thought you'd feel better if you were back in your own home."

She sagged in relief and the knot in her stomach loosened. "They'll want to come right over, or at least Mom will. Tell her not to bother, please. Let her know I'll call her soon."

"Of course. Now get some rest. I'll sort out dinner later."

He kissed her forehead, pulled the covers up to her chin and then quietly walked away, flipping off all the lights. She heard the door to his office close and she lay there alone in the darkness.

It wasn't anything she hadn't experienced before. In the evenings when Dev got home from work, he often sequestered himself in his office for a time while she watched TV or ordered in their dinner. But she hadn't felt so alone then. Because she'd known he was just in the next room and that in theory she could walk in there at any time. Only now it was as if a gulf had opened between them and he may as well be on the other side of the moon. She didn't feel as though she had the right to interrupt him.

She lay there as the haze slowly began to wear off. She braced herself for the inevitable onslaught of pain, but there was only a dull ache that signaled the aftereffects of a much worse headache than she'd experienced in at least two years.

For that matter, she hadn't been forced to take the pain medication prescribed for her headaches in months. Emotional stress, the doctor had said, was a trigger for her. The last time she'd battled frequent headaches had been when her mom and dad had briefly separated and she'd feared an eventual divorce.

It was the very last thing she or any of their family had ever imagined because it was so obvious her parents loved each other. The separation hadn't lasted long. Whatever their issues had been, they'd worked through them quickly and her dad had moved back into the apartment with her mom and they'd gone back to being the loving couple that Ashley had always witnessed.

But for the entire period of their separation, Ashley had been deeply unhappy and stressed and she'd battled headaches on a weekly basis. The doctor had counseled her on coming up with more effective ways to manage stress but Ashley had laughed. Now she realized she was as guilty as Devon had accused her of being when it came to wearing her feelings on her shoulder. She absorbed too much of the world around her and it affected her. That wasn't something she could change, could she?

She sighed. If she had any hope of not spending the next year in bed knocked out on medication, she was going to have to harden herself. She couldn't go around being a veritable sponge and reacting so emotionally to everything.

Her husband didn't love her? So what. She'd have to find a way to be happy. As Grammy always said, you make your nest now lie in it. Well, Ashley had certainly made the biggest, messiest nest of a marriage and now it was hers to wallow in.

As the medication wore off, she found it impossible to sleep. Her mind was buzzing with a mental list of everything she needed to do. Or not do. The list of things not to do was every bit as long as the list of things that needed to be done.

Learn to cook. That one popped uninvited into her head. She frowned because how did one simply learn to cook? Even Devon possessed rudimentary know-how in the kitchen. He could prepare simple dishes. She wasn't even sure she could boil water if necessary.

Okay that one should be simple enough. Pippa was a first-rate cook and it wouldn't be strange that Ashley would want to learn to cook a fabulous meal for her new husband. She could say she wanted to surprise him with a romantic meal for two.

And cooking shows. There was an entire television network devoted to cooking. Surely there was something she could watch there that would help.

Cleaning. Okay, she knew how to clean. She just didn't possess the organization skills to do it well. But she could muddle her way through it. It simply required discipline and less of a scatterbrain mentality.

She had to curb her tongue and her reactions. That should be simple enough. Smile and nod instead of shriek and wave her hands. Her mother was an expert at all the social graces but then she'd had to be with all the business functions she'd arranged and managed for her husband.

Ashley could certainly draw on the resources around her. She'd never particularly had a desire to be more like her family. She hadn't really considered that she was so different. She hadn't thought much about how she compared. Why would she? But they could help her. She just had to make sure she employed their help in a way that didn't give away the true reason for her transformation.

The door to Devon's office opened and he stepped out, looked her way and then started toward her.

"Can't sleep?" he asked. "Do you need anything?"

She shook her head and pulled the blanket closer to her chin. "I'm fine. Just getting comfortable."

He took a seat in the armchair across from the couch. Their gazes connected but she didn't look away, as tempted as she was. She couldn't keep avoiding him, no matter how desirable the prospect was.

It was hard for her because humiliation crept up her spine every time she had to face him, but eventually that would go away or she'd harden enough that it would no longer affect her. Or at least she hoped so.

"I spoke to your parents. Your mother is naturally concerned for you. She'd like you to call her when you're feeling up to it. Your father wants to see me in the morning, so if you're okay by then, I'll be out for a few hours."

"I'll be fine," she said softly. "Headache's gone. No reason for you to stay home and babysit me."

"If you need anything at all or if you begin to feel bad again, call me. I'll come home."

Hell would freeze over before she'd ever call him at work again, not that she'd tell him that. She nodded instead and sighed unhappily. So this is what her marriage boiled down to. A stilted, awkward conversation between two people who were clearly uncomfortable in each other's presence.

"Do you think you could eat something now?" Devon asked, breaking the strained silence. "What would you like?"

Deciding to take the olive branch, or perhaps create an olive branch out of a dinner offer, she shifted and pushed herself up so that her back was against the arm of the couch.

"You could cook, if you don't mind. I could sit at the bar and watch."

He looked surprised by her suggestion, but his surprise was quickly replaced by relief. He looked almost hopeful.

"That would be nice. Are you sure you're up for the noise and the light?"

Again she nodded. She hadn't talked this little since she'd been a nonverbal toddler. Her parents always swore that because she was late to talk she'd spent the rest of her life making up for lost time.

He stood and held down his hand to her. "Come on then. Bring the blanket with you if you're cold. You can sit on one of the bar stools and wrap it around you."

Hesitating only a brief moment, she slid her hand over his, enjoying the warmth of his touch. He curled his fingers around her wrist and helped her from the couch.

She stood up beside him but he waited a moment for her to get her footing.

"Okay?" he asked. "Fuzziness gone yet? I don't want you falling."

"I'm fine."

He didn't relinquish her hand as he started toward the kitchen. He guided her toward one of the stools and settled her down. He wrapped the blanket around her shoulders and tucked the ends underneath her arms.

"What's your pleasure tonight?"

He walked around to open the refrigerator, surveyed the contents and then glanced back at her.

It was probably another sign of her shortcomings that she had no idea what was or wasn't in the fridge. Heat singed her cheeks and she dropped her gaze. Tomorrow she'd take inventory. After she cleaned the house.

"Ash?"

She yanked her gaze back up. "Uh, I don't care. Honestly. I'll eat whatever."

"Oh, good. I've been dying to cook this cow's tongue before it goes bad."

She blinked for a moment before she realized he was teasing her. The memory of the night he'd first made love to her came back in a flash. The dinner they'd had when he'd asked her if she was a vegetarian.

Unbidden, a smile curved her lips. He smiled back at her, relief lightening his eyes.

"No?" he asked.

She shook her head. "No cow's tongue. But I'd eat his flank. Or his tuchus even."

"So you'll eat cow's ass but not his tongue," Devon said in mock exasperation.

Her smile grew a bit bigger and she leaned forward on the counter, resting her chin in her palm. This pretending felt nice. Who said denial was a bad thing?

If she could effectively put out of her mind the whole debacle that had been her honeymoon and take some time to work on her shortcomings, maybe at some point the pretense could become real. He could love her. He was committed to their marriage. It was a step. He was attentive, caring and he obviously hated to see her hurting. Those weren't the characteristics of a man who loathed her. So if he didn't hate her, and he seemed to like her well enough even if she annoyed him, then eventually, possibly, he could love her.

It was a hope she clung to because the alternative didn't bear thinking about. He didn't want a divorce, but she couldn't remain married to a man who could never love her. If she lost hope that he'd never reciprocate her feelings, it would signal the end of their marriage whether he wished it or not.

Devon tossed a package onto the counter and then returned

to the fridge, where he pulled out an onion, what looked like bell peppers in assorted colors and a box of mushrooms.

"How about I do stir-fry? It's quick and easy and pretty damn good if I do say so myself."

"Sounds yummy."

She watched him in silence and soon the sizzle of searing meat filled the room. While the meat cooked, he sliced the vegetables. He stopped to give the meat a brisk stirring and then returned to the cutting board.

She decided he looked good in the kitchen. Sleeves rolled up, top button undone, his brow creased in concentration. He was efficient, but then he seemed efficient at everything he did. She wondered if there was anything he wasn't accomplished at. Was he one of those people who could pick up anything and do it well?

"Name one thing you suck at," she blurted out.

Then she promptly groaned inwardly because this was precisely what she wasn't supposed to be doing. She had to demonstrate more…control. More decorum. Or at least stop blurting out her first reaction to everything.

He glanced up, his brows drawn together as if he wasn't sure if he'd heard her correctly. "Say that again?"

She shook her head. No way. "It was stupid. Just forget it."

He put down the knife, glanced over at the skillet and then returned his gaze to her. "Why would you want to know something I suck at?"

She closed her eyes and wished the floor would just open up and swallow her. So much for her campaign to become less… everything on his complaint list about her.

"Ash? Come on. Don't leave me hanging here."

She sighed. "Look, it was a stupid question. It's just that you seem like one of these people who is good at everything. You know, a person who can pick up something and just do it and do it well. I just wanted to know one thing you suck at. Gives hope to us mere mortals."

He shrugged. "I suck at lots of things. I'm definitely not one of those people who is good at everything. I've had to work hard for everything I've earned."

This was going from bad to worse. "It didn't come out right, Dev, okay? Can we just forget it? I wasn't insinuating that you haven't worked hard. I think it's evident that you've worked for everything you have. That wasn't what I meant at all. Sorry."

She pushed her hand into her hair and focused her stare down at the countertop. Running out of the room seemed overly dramatic even if it was what she wanted more than anything.

"Then what did you mean?"

There wasn't any anger or irritation in his voice. Just simple, casual curiosity. She chanced a peek back up at him to gauge his expression.

"Well, like cooking. You seem good at that. I just wanted to know something you aren't good at. You seemed to me to be one of those people who have a natural ability to pick up on things. You know, like sports. You ever see kids who just pick up a ball and know how to play? I bet you were one of those."

He groaned. "Oh, man. Clearly you've never watched me try to play basketball. And I say try, but that's probably not even an accurate word to use. Rafael, Ryan and Cam like to torture me at least once a year when they drag me down to play a 'friendly' game of basketball. What it really is is an opportunity for them to pay me back for every imagined slight. And then they don't let me forget it for the next six months."

"So you aren't good at basketball? Is that what you're saying?"

"Yeah. That's exactly what I'm saying."

She smiled. "Oh. Well, that's okay because I'm terrible at it, too."

He smiled back at her and then tossed the vegetables into the pan he'd taken the meat out of. "We can be terrible together then."

"Yeah," she said quietly.

He busied himself finishing up the meal and five minutes later, he set a plate in front of her while he stood on the other side of the bar, leaning back against the sink while he held his plate.

She looked up and frowned. "Not going to sit down?"

"I like watching you," he said as his gaze slid over her face. "I'd prefer to be across from you."

Her cheeks warmed and she quickly looked back down at her plate. She had no response for that. It puzzled her that he'd say such a thing.

But maybe he was trying. Like she was trying. Just as she would be trying as she embarked on her to do list the next day.

It wouldn't happen overnight, but maybe...one day.

Thirteen

Ashley woke with a muggy hangover feeling but then who wouldn't after two days in a medication-induced coma?

Today was the first day in her bid to take over the world. Well, sort of. Or rather it was her attempt to *not* take on the world quite so much. *Reserve* and *caution* were her two new friends.

There would be no more lying around and feeling sorry for herself.

Devon had exited the apartment early. The previous night had been a study in awkwardness.

He'd crawled into bed next to her and they'd lain quietly in the dark until finally she'd drifted off to a troubled sleep. Sometime during the night, he'd drifted toward her, or maybe she'd attacked him in her sleep. Either way, she'd ended up in his arms and had awakened when he'd gotten up early to shower.

He'd kissed her on the head and murmured for her to go back to sleep before leaving her alone.

"Welcome to your new reality," she murmured as she pushed herself out of bed.

She spent her entire time in the shower lecturing herself on how her situation was what she made of it. It could be horrible or she could salvage it. It was just according to how much effort she wanted to invest in her own happiness. Put that way, she could hardly say to hell with it and stomp off.

She winced when she caught sight of herself in the mirror. She looked bad. Not in one of those ways where she really didn't look so bad but said so anyway. She honestly looked like death warmed over. There were dark circles under her eyes. There was a line around her mouth from having her jaw set so firmly. Her unhappiness was etched on her face for the world to see. She'd never been good at hiding any kind of emotion. She was as transparent as plastic wrap.

Thank goodness for Carly and her never-ending list of tips for any type of makeup emergency. This definitely called for the full treatment.

When she was finished with her hair and makeup she was satisfied to see that at least she didn't look quite so haggard. Tired, yes, but that could easily be explained away by the headache. Surely an ecstatic new bride would smile her way through even the worst of migraines.

First stop was her mother's, since if Gloria Copeland didn't soon hear from her chick, she'd move Manhattan to get there to make sure all was well. After that was tackled, she had work to do. A lot of work.

She took a cab over to her former apartment building and smiled when Alex hurried to greet her.

"How are you, Miss Ashley? How is married life treating you?"

It was a standard question that would likely be asked of her a hundred more times before the week was out. Right after the one where most people would ask her why the hell she was back home after only two nights on her honeymoon.

"I'm good, Alex. Here to see my mother. Will you ring up and let her know I'm on my way?"

A moment later, Ashley stepped off the elevator and into the spacious apartment that very nearly occupied an entire floor. It was where she had spent a large portion of her childhood and it still felt like home to her no matter that she'd moved out on her own some time ago.

"Ashley, darling!" her mother cried as she hurried to greet her daughter. "Oh, you poor, poor darling. Come here and let me see you. Is your headache better? I knew there was simply too much excitement going on with the wedding and your moving and all the other plans. I worried it would prove to be too much for you. We should have spaced out the arrangements better."

Her mom enveloped her in a hug and for a long moment, Ashley clung to the comfort that only a mother could offer when her world was otherwise crap.

"Ashley?" her mother asked in a concerned, hushed tone when they finally pulled apart. "Is everything all right? Come, sit down. You don't even look like yourself today."

Ashley allowed herself to be pulled over to the comfortable leather couch. It smelled like home. She settled back and immediately burrowed into the corner, allowing the familiarity to surround her like a blanket.

"I'm fine, Mama. Really. I think you were right. There's been so much excitement and stress that when we finally got to St. Angelo I just crashed. Poor Devon was stuck taking care of me while I was insensible from the medication."

"As he should have. I'm glad he took good care of my baby for me. Are you feeling better now? You're pale and there are dark smudges under your eyes."

So much for Carly's awesome makeup tips.

"I'm better. I just wanted to come over so you wouldn't worry. I have to go back soon. There's a lot I need to do in our apartment to get everything squared away."

Her mom patted her on the arm. "Of course. But first, let me fix you a nice cup of hot tea."

"Spiced tea?" Ashley asked hopefully.

Her mother smiled. "With a peppermint."

Ashley sighed and relaxed into the couch, more than willing to allow her mom to fuss over her and baby her before she crawled back into the real world. If only manufacturers could package a mom's TLC into a box of bandages, they'd make millions.

Think of the marketing opportunities. Life sucks? Slap a mom bandage on and everything's instantly better.

A few minutes later, Ashley's mother returned carrying a tray that she set on the coffee table in front of Ashley. She handed her a cup of steaming tea and then unwrapped a peppermint that Ashley dropped into the bottom.

Ashley studied her mom as she settled back onto the couch, her own cup of tea in hand. "Mom? What happened between you and dad?"

Her mom reacted in surprise and cast Ashley a startled glance as she set her teacup back on its saucer. "Whatever do you mean, darling?"

"When you separated that time. I never asked because honestly I wanted to forget it ever happened. But now that I'm married... I just wanted to know. You two have always seemed so in love."

Her mother's eyes softened and she leaned forward to put her cup down on the coffee table. Then she turned and gathered Ashley's free hand in hers.

"It's natural for you to worry about those things now that you're married yourself. But darling, don't dwell on them."

"I know, but it just seems like that if it could happen to you and Daddy that it could happen to anyone. Was he having an affair? Did you forgive him?"

"Oh, good Lord, no!" She sighed and shook her head. "I know it was difficult for you and Eric, but especially for you. I never imagined that you'd think something like that, though. I should have guessed. I was so determined not to drag you children into our mess and thought I was doing the best thing by protecting you from any of the details. I can see I was wrong."

"What happened then?" Ashley asked softly.

"Oh it sounds so silly now. But back then I was convinced that my marriage was over. Your father was doing what he's always done. The difference was, suddenly it wasn't good enough for me. I began to worry. Maybe it's normal to go through a stage where you question what you want out of a relationship or worry that perhaps your partner doesn't love or value you anymore. Your father was working a lot of long hours. He was traveling constantly. You and Eric were adults and were going your own way and suddenly I found myself feeling quite alone and no longer valuable."

"Oh, Mama. I wish I had known," Ashley said unhappily. "That sounds so very awful for you."

Her mom smiled. "It was at the time but it wasn't entirely your father's fault. He was caught completely off guard when he returned home only to discover that I'd moved his things out and he had to find another place to live. He begged me to tell him what was wrong, what he'd done wrong, how he could fix it. But the truth was, I didn't even know myself. I just knew I was unhappy and that I no longer knew what I wanted from my marriage or my husband. If I didn't know, how could he?"

"What did you do?"

"I refused to speak to him for a week. It wasn't that I was angry. I just didn't know what to say to him. I took that time to think about and articulate what it was I wanted to say to him. And during that time, I realized that it wasn't him that I needed to change. It was me. I needed to find what was going to make me happy and he couldn't do it for me.

"When I finally agreed to see him, the poor man looked like death warmed over. I felt so guilty for the way I'd made him suffer but I knew we'd never last if I couldn't get myself together. I asked him for a period of separation. He was adamantly opposed. It wasn't until I gently reminded him that I didn't need his permission and that we were already separated that he backed off."

Ashley frowned. "I always assumed…I mean I just thought that it was Daddy's decision to move out. I always wondered if there was another woman."

Her mom twisted her lips in a regretful frown. "Yes, it's what Eric thought too, unfortunately. He was furious with your father. It wasn't until I explained things to him that he calmed down. Then I think he was angry with me for making your father move out. Eric is very black-and-white."

"Yes, I know," Ashley said with a grimace. She took another sip of her tea and then looked back at her mom. "So what happened? What made you decide to let him move back in?"

Her mom sighed and a faraway look entered her eyes. "We were separated for six months and in a way, those six months were some of the best times of my life."

Ashley's eyes widened. "But Mama!"

"I know, I know, but listen to me. I didn't say they were easy. They weren't. But those six months outlined to me in clear detail what I wanted my life to be. And who I wanted to spend it with. I had opportunities. There were plenty of men who flirted with me and would have jumped at the opportunity to date or have an affair."

Ashley's mouth dropped open and her mother smiled at her reaction. "Darling, you don't think the need for sex goes away when you hit thirty, do you?"

"Oh, my God," Ashley muttered. "I'm so not hearing my mother talk about all the hot guys she had a chance with while she was separated from my father."

"I had opportunity, yes, but I couldn't do it," her mom said.

"Because you loved Daddy?"

"Because it would have been dishonorable. Your father didn't deserve it. Because I honestly didn't want to be with anyone other than him. And I realized that I'd been blaming him for my own unhappiness. It was easy to say he'd been neglecting me or that he spent too much time at work. But the truth was, after you children grew up and left the nest, I simply didn't know what it was I wanted to do next. And I took out my frustrations on the closest available target because I didn't want to take responsibility for my own failures and feelings of inadequacy."

"Wow, I never realized…"

Her mom smiled and reached up to touch her cheek. "What, that I'm human like everyone else? That your mom isn't perfect?"

"Well, yeah, I guess," Ashley said lamely. "It's a totally shocking discovery. You may not survive the fall from the mom pedestal."

Her mom laughed and tweaked Ashley's nose. "Such a smart alec like your father. I always thought you were so much like him."

"What? I'm nothing like Daddy. He'd probably be horrified to hear you say that. He despairs of me because I have no head for or interest in business."

Her mom smiled indulgently. "But you have a huge heart like your father does and when you love, you love with everything you have. Just like William. He was devastated when I asked him to leave. And even though I knew I absolutely had to do what I did, it was the most difficult decision I've ever made. Our marriage is better for it. When we got back together, I was a stronger, more confident woman. I didn't need him to make me complete. I wanted him. But I didn't need him and therein was the difference."

Ashley set aside her cup and then impulsively threw her arms around her mom in a hug. "I love you, Mama. Thank you for talking to me. It was just what I needed today."

Her mother stroked her hand over Ashley's hair and hugged

her back. "You're welcome, darling, and I love you, too. You know I'm always right here if you need me."

Devon sat across from William Copeland as William completed his order with the waitress. The two had met at William's favorite place to eat lunch, but Devon wasn't in the least bit hungry.

"You not eating, son?" William asked as the waitress looked expectantly in Devon's direction.

"I'll just have a glass of water," Devon said.

After the waitress left, William leaned back and for a moment looked visibly discomfited.

"I wanted to talk to you about some changes in the organization."

Alarm bells clanged in Devon's already aching head. Two nights without decent sleep and the image of Ashley's tearstained face were wearing on him. The very last thing he needed was the old man to renege on their agreement. Wouldn't that be the height of irony?

He must have seen the wariness on Devon's face because he quickly went on.

"It's not what you think. I want you to take over my position at Copeland. I know the merger with Tricorp wasn't supposed to be splashy, that we agreed to keep the Copeland name and that Tricorp would be more of a silent party, but I'm ready to resign and I want you to take my position."

Devon shook his head in confusion. "I don't understand."

William sighed wearily. "I'm sick, son. I've been having health issues. I've been trying to see to matters because I want my family provided for. I want Eric to have a position but he isn't ready to take over. And the thing is, I'm not sure he wants his future locked into the family business. Lately he's hinted that his interests lie in other areas. And Ashley... It's why I pushed so hard for the marriage to take place. I wanted her settled with a man I trusted and whom I knew would take good care of her. If it got out that my health was failing, the vultures would have descended and she would have been easy pickings."

"Sick?" Devon managed to get out. "How sick?"

"I don't know yet. I won't lie. I've been in denial. I haven't even discussed this with Gloria and she's going to hit the ceiling when she finds out. I'm not ready to die yet, though. I want a lot of years with my children and eventual grandchildren. I spent decades working my ass off to get where I am and now I want to retire and enjoy time with my wife and watch my grandchildren play. But in order to do all that, I have to make sure my company is in good hands. I don't want Copeland to die, which is why I wanted this merger so badly. It wasn't Tricorp I was after. To be honest I could have picked a dozen other companies who would bring as much to the table. But I went with Tricorp because of you. You're who I want for my daughter and my company."

"Jesus, I don't even know what to say," Devon muttered. "This is quite the bomb to drop the day after I return from an aborted honeymoon."

"I know you thought I was a crazy old man for making Ashley part of this deal. And that I'm a manipulative bastard. You'd be right on that count. I knew you wanted this partnership. I knew you wanted the Copeland name for the line of resorts you've envisioned. I also knew what I wanted. It just so happened that our wants aligned perfectly. And my children are provided for."

"Everyone but Ashley," Devon said quietly.

William looked up sharply. "What do you mean?"

"She wanted a husband who adores her, who loves her, who is the embodiment of all she's dreamed of."

"So? Any reason you can't be that man?"

It was a good question and one he wasn't sure how to answer. He rubbed his hand through his hair. "How soon are you wanting all of this done?"

"I want to tender my resignation as soon as everything is done. It won't be a secret that I'll want you to take over. Voting won't be an issue. You'll be the most logical person to take over when I retire. I hold a lot of sway over the board. They'll listen to me. I'm going to make a doctor's appointment and then tell my wife so she can rearrange my teeth for me and then drag me to the doctor. After that, she'll take over and I won't be able to scratch my ass without her permission."

The words were said with wry wit, but it was obvious from the warmth in William's eyes that he adored his wife beyond reason and absolutely didn't mind giving up control to her in his retirement.

The older man seemed totally at peace with his actions and decisions and Devon wondered how much he could really fault his father-in-law for taking steps to ensure that his family was provided for. Even if he didn't agree with the methods. Would he have done the same for his son or daughter?

He liked to think that he'd offer them something better than the occasional reminder not to "screw up."

The image of Ashley, round and lush with his child, conjured a powerful surge of emotion. He realized in an instant that he'd do whatever it took to protect a son or daughter.

"Take care of yourself," Devon said gruffly, suddenly unsteady at the idea of something happening to a man who'd seemed so determined to be a second father to him. "I'll expect you to spoil our children."

William's expression eased into a broad smile. "Planning to provide me with them soon?"

Devon shrugged. "Maybe. That'll be up to Ash. I just want her to be happy."

William nodded. "So do I, son. So do I."

They were interrupted by the waitress bringing William's entrée to the table. For a moment, William fussed over his food and then he looked up at Devon again. "I'd like you to plan a cocktail party. It'll give Ashley a chance to play hostess. I'm thinking a couple weeks out at most. I want to go ahead and announce that I'm planning to retire and that you're my choice to succeed me. I want this all to seem like a natural progression of the merger. A changing of the guard with my blessing."

"We can do that," Devon said. Or at least he hoped. Maybe by that time Ashley wouldn't be quite so upset. Right now, asking her to appear happy for an entire night in front of dozens of guests seemed unreasonable at best.

"Good. We'll talk more later and I'll give you a guest list and of course you'll have your own colleagues to invite. I just want to say again how happy I am to have you as my son-in-law. I knew from the moment I met you that you'd not only be the best thing for my company, but for my daughter as well."

Fourteen

When Devon walked into his apartment, he immediately noticed the change. There wasn't any clutter. No magazines strewn about. No shoes littering the floor. No purse hanging from a doorknob. And he could smell cleaning solution.

As he walked farther inside, his stomach knotted because not only was everything picked up, but he also realized that the apartment was completely and utterly devoid of Ashley's presence. All of the things she'd moved in and haphazardly decorated with had been put away. No silly knickknacks on the coffee or end tables.

The apartment looked precisely as it had before she moved in.

Has she packed up and left? Had she decided not to give their marriage a chance?

He experienced a faint sensation of illness. His stomach tightened with dread and the beginnings of panic gripped his throat.

Then he heard a distant sound that seemed to come from

the kitchen. He strode in that direction and realized that a television had been left on. But when he reached the doorway, he had to grip the frame to steady himself.

Relief blew through him with staggering ferocity.

She was still here.

She hadn't left.

She was sitting at the bar, her brow furrowed in concentration as she watched a cooking show. She had a notepad and pencil in front of her and she was furiously taking notes.

As his gaze took in the rest of the kitchen, he realized that she'd evidently spent the day cleaning. The surfaces sparkled. The floor shone. The scent of lemon was heavy in the air.

She was dressed in faded jeans and an old T-shirt. Her hair was pulled back into a ponytail and she wasn't wearing any makeup.

She looked absolutely beautiful.

But she also looked tired. The dark circles under her eyes were more pronounced and she had a delicate fragileness to her that made him instinctively protective of her. But he couldn't protect her from himself and it was he who had hurt her.

Drawn to the vulnerable image she presented, he slid his hands up her arms and then lowered his mouth to kiss her on the neck.

She froze immediately then turned swiftly around. "Hi," she offered hesitantly. "I didn't expect you back quite so soon."

"Technically I'm off this week," he said as he pulled away. "I had lunch with your father. We discussed business and now I'm done."

She made a face but didn't comment, which he was grateful for. Anytime her father and business were mentioned, it was going to be difficult, but the more he did it in passing, maybe it would lessen the sting.

"What happened to all your stuff?" he asked casually as he went around to open the fridge. He pulled out a bottle of water and pushed the door closed.

"Oh, I just organized everything," she said. "I didn't really have time before the wedding. Was too busy with other stuff."

"Mmm-hmm," he murmured. "And the cleaning? Should you have been doing all this today? You just came off a pretty bad headache. I wouldn't think all the cleaning stuff would be good for you to be inhaling."

"It was okay. Headache is gone. Just a little residual achiness."

He frowned. "Why don't you go lie on the couch. I'll figure out dinner and we'll watch some TV or just relax in the living room if you don't want the noise."

She rose from the stool. "No, no, I've got dinner planned. Are you hungry already? What time did you want to eat?"

Perplexed by her sudden agitation, he hastily backed off. It appeared she was at least trying for a semblance of normalcy and that relieved him. Maybe after the initial storm passed and she had time to think she'd see that nothing had changed between them.

In light of today's conversation with William Copeland, Devon was on the verge of accomplishing all his goals. And at a much faster rate than he'd ever planned. Five years down the road was here now. Copeland Hotels would be his. His dream of launching a new luxury chain of exclusive resorts under one of the oldest and most respected names in the business would be realized. He'd have a wife. Children. A family. He'd have it all.

The surge of triumph was so forceful he felt drunk with it.

"I'm in no hurry," he soothed. "Why don't we sit down and have a drink. What are you cooking?"

A dull flush worked over her face. "I'm not. At least not tonight I mean. I will another time. I thought I'd call for takeout. It's almost like a home-cooked meal but they bring it and set it up."

"Sounds wonderful. Thank you. I think a nice quiet dinner at home would be fantastic after the week we've had. We didn't really get to see each other much in the days leading up to the wedding. We can start making up for that now."

Pain flashed in her eyes but she remained quiet, almost as if she was dealing with the sudden reminder of their circumstances. He hated it. Wished he could wipe it from her memory. In time, it would fade. If he showed her that they could have a comfortable relationship, some of the rawness of her emotions would settle and they could go back to the easy camaraderie they'd shared before everything went to hell.

She squared her shoulders as if reaching a decision and then tilted her chin upward. "You go on out and have a seat. Would you like wine? Or do you want me to mix up something for you?"

He opened his mouth to tell her that he'd take care of it, but something in her eyes stopped him. There was a quiet desperation, almost as if she was barely clinging to her composure.

"Wine would be great," he said softly. "You choose something for both of us. I like everything I've stocked here so I'm good with whatever you pick out."

He left the kitchen, his chest tight. The next weeks were going to suck as they found their way in the new reality of their relationship. He had confidence that it would work out, though. He just had to be patient.

A few minutes later, Ashley came into the living room carrying two wineglasses and a bottle of unopened wine. She looked disgruntled as she set the glasses down on the coffee table.

"Can you open the wine?" she asked hesitantly. "I couldn't get the bottle opener to work properly. I'm sure I'm not doing it right."

He reached for the bottle and let his fingers glide over hers. "Relax, Ash. Take a seat. I'll pour."

Reluctantly she backtracked and sank down onto the couch. In truth she still didn't look well and it wouldn't surprise him if her head was still hurting her. Her brow was wrinkled and she looked tired. Maybe a glass of wine would ease some of her tension.

He opened the bottle and then poured a glass for her first. After pouring his own, he set the glass on the table and took a seat in the armchair diagonal to where she sat on the couch.

"Your father wants us to host a cocktail party in a week or two," he said.

"Us?" she squeaked. "As in you and me? Why wouldn't he want Mama to host it? She's awesome at hosting parties. Everyone always talks about how much fun they have when she throws a get-together."

"He's going to be announcing some changes at Copeland soon and this is his way of easing into that. Your father is looking at taking a less active role in the managing of things. He's ready to retire and focus on his family."

She looked despondent.

"Ash, this isn't a big deal. Most of the people who'll attend are people we already know. We'll pick a nice venue, have it catered, hire a band. It'll be great."

She held up her hand. "I'll handle it. No problem. I don't want you to worry about it. I just need to know exactly when. I'm sure you and Daddy will be busy with…whatever it is you're busy with. Mama always handled parties for Daddy. No reason I can't do it for you."

The dismay in her voice troubled him. He thought it rather sounded like she would be planning a funeral, but he wasn't about to shut her down when she was making such an effort. That she was so willing to try when it was obvious he'd crushed her endeared her to him all the more.

"I'm sure whatever you come up with, I and the others will love," he said.

She took a long drink of her wine, nearly draining the glass.

"Want to watch a movie?" he suggested.

She nodded as she put her wineglass back on the coffee table. "Sure. Whatever you want to put on is fine."

He picked up the remote but he didn't return to his own chair. He eased onto the couch next to her and put his arm along the top of the sofa behind her head.

For a long moment she sat there stiffly, almost as if she wasn't sure what she was supposed to do. He cursed the awkwardness between them. Before she wouldn't have hesitated to burrow underneath him and snuggle in tight. She'd drape herself over him when they watched movies. She would have kissed him, hugged him and generally mauled him with affection through the entire show.

Now she sat beside him like a statue, tension and fatigue radiating from her like a beacon.

"Come here," he murmured, pulling her underneath his arm. "That's better," he said when she finally relaxed against him and laid her cheek on his chest.

They were silent as the movie played and he was fine with that. There wasn't a lot he could say. There were only so many times he could apologize or tell her he hadn't meant to hurt her.

It wasn't the movie that captured his attention, though. He sat there enjoying her scent. Her hair always smelled like honeysuckle. Even in winter in the city. She had an airy, floral scent that clung to her. It suited her.

And he loved the feel of her next to him. He hadn't realized how much until he'd spent the last several days with a wall between them.

He touched her hair, idly sifting through the strands with his fingers, savoring the sensation of silk over his skin. By the time the credits rolled, he couldn't have even said what the movie was about. He hadn't cared.

"Ash, are you sure you don't want me to go out for some dinner?" He waited a moment. "Ash?"

He glanced down to see that she'd fallen sound asleep against his chest. Her lashes rested delicately on her cheeks and her lips were tight, almost as if she were deep in thought even at rest.

Gently he kissed her forehead and rested his chin there for a long moment. Somehow, someway, he would make it up to her. He was reaching the high point in his life and career where everything he'd worked so hard and so long for was his. And damn it, he wanted her to be on top of the world with him.

Fifteen

"This is hopeless," Ashley said as her shoulders sagged.

Pippa wrapped her arm around Ashley and squeezed tight. "You're not hopeless. You'll get it down. You're being way too hard on yourself."

"After three weeks, you'd think I'd be able to perform the simplest tasks in the kitchen," Ashley said forlornly. "Let's face it. I'm a culinary disaster."

"Are you all right, hon? You seem really down lately and not just about this cooking stuff. Is everything okay with you?"

Ashley smiled brightly and straightened her stance. "Oh, yeah, fine. Marriage is exhausting work. Who knew? Just trying to get my routine down. I've been spending my mornings at the shelter so I can be at home when Devon gets in from work. I keep hoping one of my meals will actually turn out but I keep having to call in backup."

Pippa laughed. "You're so silly. I don't even know why you're bothering learning to cook. Devon doesn't care if you can cook. The man's obviously crazy about you and you couldn't cook before you got married. I'm sure he's not expecting some miracle to occur."

Ashley bit her lip to keep from crying. The truth was, she was exhausted. Planning that damn cocktail party had turned out to be a giant pain in her ass. She was tempted to call her mother and beg for help but pride kept her from making that call.

The old Ashley would have laughed, thrown her hands up and admitted she was hopeless. The new Ashley was going to suck it up, be calm and get the job done.

"Are you coming to my party?" Ashley asked, suddenly worried she'd be surrounded by a sea of unfamiliar faces.

"Of course I am. I promised you I'd come. I know you're nervous, but really, this is your thing, Ash. You shine at social events. Everyone loves you and you're so sweet."

"Why don't you meet me at Tabitha's place the afternoon before. We'll get our hair done together. I'm aiming for a more sophisticated look for the party. You know, mature and married as opposed to young and flighty."

Pippa snorted. "Flighty?"

Ashley laughed it off but she knew well that Devon considered her a complete ditz.

"I need Carly's makeup skills, too."

"Honey, you aren't holding tea for the queen. You're hosting a cocktail party for friends and business associates. We already love you. And those who don't will. Stop tormenting yourself over this."

"I just don't want to look stupid," Ashley said.

Pippa shook her head. "I swear I don't know what's got into you lately. You're perfect and anyone who doesn't think so can kiss my ass."

"I love you," Ashley said, emotion knotting her throat.

Pippa hugged her fiercely and then pulled away. "Are you pregnant or something? I swear you're not usually so emotional."

"Oh, God, I don't think so. I mean it's possible but I haven't even kept up with my periods. I just remember being thrilled it wasn't going to happen on my honeymoon. You know, the one I ended up cutting short."

"Well, take one of those home pregnancy tests. You're a mess, Ash. Hormones have to be the reason why."

She closed her eyes. No, she couldn't be pregnant yet. Well, she certainly could, but she suddenly didn't want to be. But it was a little too late for that line of thinking. When was the last time she and Devon had made love anyway? Definitely before the wedding. But it was still too soon to tell.

"I'll give it a little more time," she said firmly. "I'm just a wreck over this stupid party. I feel like it's my first big test as Mrs. Devon Carter. I don't want to humiliate myself or him in front of a hundred people."

"Stop it," Pippa chided. "You're going to be awesome. Now, do you want to try this sauce again?"

Ashley sighed. "I'm thinking I should start out with something even easier. Sauces aren't my thing apparently. I keep ruining them."

"Okay, then let's try something different. Name something else you love to eat."

Ashley thought a minute. "Lasagna. That sounds really good right now."

"Perfect! And it couldn't be easier. I'll give you the easy recipe. You can always graduate to fancier once you've mastered the kid-friendly version."

"That's me," Ashley said in resignation. "The kid-friendly version."

Pippa swatted her with a towel. "Grab the hamburger meat from the fridge. I think we're down to the last pack so you better nail this one, girlfriend."

Half an hour later, Ashley put her fist in the air as she and Pippa stood back and closed the oven door on a perfect, if somewhat beleaguered, lasagna.

"I can totally do that on my own," Ashley said as Pippa wiped her hands. "I'm so excited! Maybe I'm not a complete lost cause."

Pippa shook her head. "All it takes is a little time and patience. You're going to be a culinary genius in no time."

Ashley threw her arms around her friend and hugged her tight. "Thanks, Pip. I love you, you know. You're the best."

Pippa grinned. "I love you, too, you nut. Now go home and make your lasagna before your husband gets there. Call me tomorrow and let me know how it went. And take that damn pregnancy test. I'll want to know if I'm going to be an aunt!"

Ashley rolled her eyes. She started to walk toward the door when her cell phone beeped, signaling a received text message. She pulled it out and then frowned as she read it.

"What is it, Ash?" Pippa asked.

"There's a problem at the shelter. Molly is upset but she doesn't give any info. I'll hop over on my way home. It's not too out of the way. See you Friday afternoon at Tabitha's."

"Okay, be careful and call me when you get home so I'll know you made it. You know I hate you going down to the shelter by yourself all the time."

"Yes, mother," Ashley replied. "Later, chickie."

With a wave, she disappeared from Pippa's apartment and headed down to catch a cab to the shelter.

It was later than he'd have liked when Devon entered the apartment. His day had been long and full of endless meetings and his ears were still throbbing from the number of people who'd talked to him.

The only person he wanted to see was Ashley, and he was looking forward to seeing what disaster she'd come up with for dinner.

He grinned as he loosened his tie and headed for the kitchen. The past weeks had been hilarious. Oddly, he hadn't minded the sheer number of ruined meals he'd been served. It had become a contest for him to correctly guess what the meal was *supposed* to have been.

He sniffed as he reached the doorway into the kitchen and the delicious aroma of…something…floated into his nostrils. It didn't smell burned. Or even slightly scorched. It smelled like gooey, bubbly cheese and a hint of tomato.

His stomach growled and he scanned the kitchen area for Ashley. He frowned when he realized she was nowhere to be seen. Deciding he'd better check on whatever was for dinner, he hurried to the oven and pulled open the door.

Inside was what looked to be a perfectly put together and perfectly cooked lasagna. He snagged a potholder and then reached inside to take out the casserole dish.

After setting it on the stove, he turned off the oven and then went in search of Ashley. As he neared the bedroom, he heard the low murmur of her voice.

She was standing by the window overlooking the city and she was on her cell phone. He started to detour into his closet to change when he heard a betraying sniff.

He spun around, frowning as he zeroed in on Ashley. Her back was mostly to him though she was angled just enough that he could see her wipe at one cheek.

What the hell?

It took all his restraint not to walk over, take the phone and demand to know who the hell had upset her.

"I'll see what I can do, Molly. We can't let this happen," she said.

She wiped her cheek with the back of her free hand and then hit the button to end the call. Then she turned and saw Devon. Her eyes widened in alarm and then she closed them in dismay.

"Oh, my God, the lasagna!"

She bolted for the door, gone before he could even tell her he'd already taken care of it. He was more concerned with what had made her cry.

"Ash!" he called as he hurried after her.

He caught up to her in the kitchen to find her palming her forehead as she stared at the lasagna.

"I'm sorry," she said. "I just forgot it. If you hadn't come in, it would have burned."

"Hey, it's okay," he said. He walked over and slipped a hand over her shoulder. "It needs to rest a minute anyway. Let me grab some plates and we'll set the table. Then you can tell me what's got you so upset. Who was that on the phone?"

He steered her toward the table, parked her in a chair and then went back to retrieve plates and utensils. After setting the places, he went back for the lasagna and carried the still piping hot dish to the table.

He sat down, picking up a knife to cut into the lasagna while he waited for her to respond. To his horror, her eyes filled with tears and she buried her face in her hands.

He dropped the knife and bit out a curse. Then he scrambled out of his chair and pulled it around so he could scoot up next to Ashley.

"What's wrong?" he demanded. "Did someone upset you?" Obviously someone or something did but he wanted answers. He wasn't a patient man. His inclination was to wade in and fix things. He couldn't do that if he didn't have the story.

"I've had the most awful day," she croaked out. "And I wanted everything to be perfect. I finally learned how to cook that damn lasagna. But then Molly called. I stopped by the shelter and she had terrible news and I don't know what to do. We've been talking about it all evening."

He gently pulled her hands away, wincing at the flood of tears soaking her cheeks.

"Who's Molly?"

She frowned and lifted her gaze to meet his. "Molly from the shelter."

He looked searchingly at her. Clearly this was a person he was supposed to know, but he was drawing a complete blank.

"She's my boss at the shelter."

"Wait a minute. I thought you ran the shelter."

She shook her head impatiently. "I do, mostly, but she's in charge. I mean she runs it but I do most of the legwork and fundraising. She says I have more connections and am the natural choice to go out and pound the pavement for donations."

Devon scowled. It sounded to him as though this Molly person was taking advantage of Ashley. He wasn't certain of the salary that Ashley drew from her position at the shelter. He assumed that her parents still helped her financially since she didn't have a typical nine-to-five job and she'd been living in her own apartment for a while now. He hadn't concerned himself with her finances because he wanted her to be happy and he knew he'd fully support her once they were married. But he sure as hell didn't want her busting her ass in a job where she was being used.

"So what did Molly have to say?" he gently prompted.

"The grant the shelter had is being pulled and without it, we can't continue to stay open. It pays the basics like the utilities, food for the animals and the salary for the vet we have on retainer. We don't raise enough money to stay afloat without the grant."

Her eyes filled with tears again. "If we don't stay open, all the animals will have to be transferred to a city-run shelter and if they aren't adopted out, they'll be euthanized."

Devon sighed and carefully pulled Ashley into his arms. "Surely there's some way to keep the shelter open. Have you talked to your father about sponsoring it?"

She pulled away and shook her head. "You don't understand. Daddy's all business when it comes to stuff like that. He doesn't make emotional decisions. He's more interested in profit and return or it being a cause he sees the value in. He's not much of an animal person."

Ashley's view of her father was clearly wrong. William Copeland had made an emotional decision. A huge emotional decision when he'd opted to go with Tricorp because for whatever reason he'd decided Devon would be the perfect son-in-law and candidate to take over Copeland.

"How long can you continue running as you are now?"

She sniffed. "Two, maybe three weeks. I'm not sure. We're already at maximum capacity but it's hard to say no when a new animal comes in. We just got in a dog and it was so heartbreaking. The poor thing is the sweetest dog ever but he was horribly neglected. I don't understand how people can be so cruel. Would they dump their child out on the street somewhere? A pet isn't any different. They're just as much a family member as a child!"

Unfortunately, there were people who'd think nothing of tossing out their kid, not that Ashley needed to be reminded of that. It would only upset her further.

He smoothed his hand over her cheek and then leaned forward to kiss her forehead. "Why don't you eat something. The lasagna smells wonderful. There's nothing you can do tonight. Maybe a solution will present itself in the morning."

She nodded morosely and he scooted his seat back. He picked the knife back up and cut into the lasagna, spooning out neat squares onto the plates.

"This looks wonderful," he said in a cheerful tone. He wanted her to smile again. She'd been entirely too serious ever since they returned from their honeymoon and he was becoming impatient for her to return to her usual, sunny self.

He handed her a plate and then took his own. When he bit into the gooey cheese and the perfectly al dente noodles, and the savory sauce slid over his tongue, he moaned in pleasure.

"This is awesome, Ash."

She smiled but it didn't quite reach her eyes. There was still deep sadness in those big, blue eyes and it was twisting his gut into a knot.

As good as dinner was, he was anxious to get through it. He had a sudden urge to comfort Ashley and wipe away her pain.

She picked at her food and it was obvious she had no interest in eating, so he hurriedly gulped his down and then collected their plates to dump into the sink. "Come here," he said, holding his hand out to her.

She slid her fingers into his and he pulled her to her feet. He took her into the bedroom, sat her on the edge of the bed and began taking her shoes off.

Crouching between her legs, he slid his hands along the sides of her thighs until his fingers palmed her hips. He held her there, staring intently at her, unable to believe he was about to make her a promise.

The business side of him balked and demanded to know if he'd lost his damn mind. But the side of him that cringed upon witnessing Ashley's distress was urging him on.

"Listen to me," he said, before he could talk himself out of it. "Let me see what I can do, okay? Don't give up hope just yet. We have a few weeks. I may be able to help."

To his surprise she threw her arms around him and hugged him fiercely. It was the first spontaneous show of affection he'd been treated to since before their marriage.

"Oh, Devon, thank you," she whispered fiercely. "You have no idea how much this would mean to me."

"I have an idea," he said wryly. "You love those animals more than you love people."

She nodded solemnly, not in the least bit abashed to admit it. Then she kissed him full on the mouth.

It was like baiting a hungry lion. He didn't wait for her to pull back in regret. Didn't offer her the chance to change her mind. He'd suffered three long weeks wanting her with every breath and knowing she was emotionally out of reach.

If this was his chance to have her back in his bed without a wealth of space between them, he was going to grab the opportunity with both hands.

He kissed her back, his hands going to her face, holding her there as he fed hungrily on her lips. Tentatively her arms circled his neck and she leaned into him with a soft, sweet sigh that tightened every one of his muscles and made him instantly hard.

He had to force himself to exercise some restraint because what he really wanted to do was tear her clothes off, haul her up the bed and make love to her until neither of them could walk.

"You have far too many clothes on," he said, near desperation as he fumbled with the buttons on her blouse. It was expensive. Probably silk. But ah, hell, he'd buy her another one.

The sound of the material rending and the buttons popping and scattering on the floor only spurred his excitement. He fumbled clumsily with the button on her pants and then began pulling to get them off her. She lifted her bottom just enough that he could slide the material down her legs and then there she was, sitting so dainty and beautiful, clad only in her pale, pink lingerie.

She was the most beautiful sight he'd ever seen. Hair tousled just enough to make her look sexy. Her lips swollen from his kiss. Eyes glazed with passion instead of deep sadness. And her skin. So soft, glowing in the lamplight. Curvy in all the right places. Generous breasts, straining at the lace cups, and hips and behind just the right size for his hands to grip.

He stood only long enough to strip out of his clothes. It wasn't practiced or smooth. He felt like a fifteen-year-old getting his first glimpse of a naked woman. If he wasn't careful, he'd be acting just like one, too.

She stared shyly up at him and he nearly groaned. "Baby, you have to stop looking at me like that. I'm holding on to my control by my fingertips and you're not helping."

She smiled then, an adorable, sweet smile that took his breath away. He forgot all about trying to maintain an air of civility. His inner caveman came barreling out, grunting and pounding his chest and muttering unintelligible words.

He swept her into his arms, hauling her back on the bed.

They landed with a soft bounce and he claimed her mouth, wanting to taste her again and again.

"Love the lingerie," he said hoarsely. "I'll love it more when it's off, though."

She wiggled beneath him and he realized she was trying to work out of her straps.

"Oh, no, let me," he breathed.

He pushed himself off her and then maneuvered himself upward so he straddled her body, his knees digging into the mattress on either side of her hips.

Her gaze slid downward to his groin and her eyes darkened. Tentatively she moved her hands slowly toward his straining erection. Color dusted her cheeks and she glanced hastily upward, almost as if she was seeking his permission to touch him.

Hell, he'd give her anything in the world if she'd touch him. He'd buy her twenty damn shelters if that would make her happy. Right now, it would make him delirious if she just wrapped those soft little fingers...

He closed his eyes and groaned as she did exactly what he'd fantasized about. Her touch was gentle. Light and tentative. Like the tips of butterfly wings dancing over his length.

She grew bolder, stroking more firmly, running the length of him with her palm until he was little more than a babbling, incoherent fool. He was supposed to be in control here. She was the innocent. He was the one with more experience. But she literally and figuratively held him in the palm of her hand.

If he didn't put an end to her inquisitive exploration, he'd find release on her belly and he wanted to be inside her more than he wanted to breathe.

Leaning down, her kissed the shallow indention between her breasts and then nuzzled the swell as he reached up to slide the straps over her shoulders.

He loved the way she smelled. It was one thing he missed about the apartment now. Before she had little bowls of potpourri and little scented candles haphazardly arranged throughout. The entire apartment had smelled like…her. Fresh. Vibrant. Like spring sunshine.

Now that she'd gone through in a mad cleaning rush, it was as if her very presence had been expunged.

The cup of her bra slipped over her nipple, exposing the puckered point to his seeking lips. He sucked lightly, enjoying the sensation of her on his tongue. Underneath him, she quivered and her breathing sped up in reaction.

He slipped one hand beneath her back, reaching for the clasp of her bra. Seconds later, it came free and he pulled carefully until it came completely away. Tossing it aside, he eyed the feast before him.

She had beautiful breasts. Just the perfect size. Small and dainty, much like her, but there was just enough plumpness to make a man's mouth water. Her nipples were a succulent pink that just beckoned him to taste. He knew enough about her now to know her breasts were highly sensitive. And her neck. Up high, just below her ear. It was guaranteed to drive her crazy if he nibbled either spot.

Tonight he wanted to taste all of her, though. He wanted her imprinted on his tongue, his senses. He wanted to be able to fall asleep smelling her, the feel of her skin on his.

Palming both breasts, he caressed, rubbed his thumbs across the tips before lowering his head to suck at one and then the other. He nipped lightly, causing the peak to harden even further. Then he slid his mouth down her middle to the softness of her belly, where he licked a damp circle around her navel.

Chill bumps rose and danced their way across her rib cage. She stirred restlessly, murmuring what sounded like a plea for more.

He thumbed the thin lace band of her panties and carefully eased the delicate material over her hips then down her legs and over her feet. Finally, she was completely naked to his avid gaze.

He moved back over her, his head hovering over the soft nest of blond curls between her legs. Then he stroked his hands over her hips and downward. He spread her thighs with firm hands, opening her to his advances.

All that pink, glistening flesh beckoned. He lowered his mouth, pressed his lips to the soft folds and nuzzled softly until she strained upward to meet him.

"Devon," she whispered.

It had been a while since he'd heard her husky sweet voice murmur his name in what was a blend of pleasure and a plea for more. It made him all the more determined that before he was finished, she'd call out his name a dozen more times. She'd find her release with his name on her lips. There would be no doubt in her mind who possessed her.

He licked gently at the tiny nub surrounded by silken folds, enjoying every jitter and shudder that rolled through her body. She was more than ready to take him, but he held back, enjoying his sensual exploration of her most intimate flesh.

Slowly he worked downward until he tasted the very heart of her, stroking with lazy, seductive swipes of his tongue. She began to shake uncontrollably and her thighs tightened around his head. He pressed one last kiss to the mouth of her opening and then moved up her body, positioning himself between her legs.

He found her heat and sank inside her with one powerful thrust. Her chin went up, her eyes closed and her lips tightened in an expression that was almost agonizing.

He kissed the dimple in her chin and then slid his mouth down her neck and to the delicate hollow of her throat. Her pulse beat wildly, jumping against her pale skin, a staccato against his mouth.

Her slender arms went around him, gripping with surprising strength. Her nails dug into his shoulders like kitten claws.

"Put your legs around me," he said. "Just like that, baby. Perfect."

She crossed her heels at the small of his back and arched into each thrust. Her fingers danced their way across his back, sometimes light and then scoring his flesh when he thrust again. She thrust one hand into his hair, pulling forcefully until he realized she was demanding his kiss.

With a light chuckle, he gave in to her silent demand and found her mouth.

Breathless. Sweet. Their tongues worked hotly over each other, dueling, fighting for dominance. She had suddenly become the aggressor and he was lost, unable to deny her anything.

She was wrapped around him, her body urging him on, arching to meet him and finding a perfect rhythm so they moved as one.

Sex had never been this...perfect.

"Are you close?" he choked out.

"Don't stop," she begged.

"Oh hell, I'm not."

He closed his eyes and thrust hard and deep. And then he began working his hips against hers in rapid, urgent movements. She let out a strangled cry and he remembered his vow.

"My name," he said in a breathless pant. "Say my name."

"Devon!"

She came apart in his arms. Around him. Underneath him. He was bathed in liquid heat and he'd never felt anything so damn good in his life.

"Ashley," he whispered. "My Ashley. Mine."

He unraveled at light speed, his release sharp, bewildering and beautiful. His hips were still convulsively moving against her body as he settled down over her, too exhausted and spent to remember his own name. The one he'd demanded she say just moments ago.

He became aware of gentle caresses. Her hands gently stroking over his back. He was probably crushing her but he couldn't bring himself to move. He was inside her. Over her. Completely covering her. She was his.

He knew this moment was significant. Something had changed. But his mind was too numb to sort out the meaning. Never before had he been so undone after making love to a woman.

It was supremely satisfying and scary as hell.

Sixteen

Ashley surveyed the guests as they filtered into the upscale restaurant she'd rented out for the night and felt the ache inside her head bloom more rapidly. She was so nervous she wanted to puke. She wanted everything to be perfect and for things to go off without a hitch.

She'd spent the afternoon at Tabitha's getting hair and makeup done. Her friends had been skeptical of the look she wanted but in the end they hadn't argued and then told her how fabulous she looked.

Ashley wanted…sophisticated. Something that didn't scream flighty, exuberant or impulsive. This was her night to prove to Devon that she was the consummate hostess and perfect complement to him.

Her dress was, as she'd been assured, the perfect little black dress. Ridiculous as it sounded, it was the first such dress that Ashley had owned. For Ashley, wearing black was the equivalent of going to a funeral. It made her feel subdued and swal-

lowed up. Somber. She much preferred brighter, more cheerful colors.

As for her hair, she never paid much attention to it and wore
it down more often than not, or she just flipped it up in a clip
and went on her way.

But Tabitha had spent an hour fashioning an elegant knot,
without a hair out of place. Pippa had grumbled that it made
her look forty and not the young twenty-something she was.

Carly had applied light makeup using muted shades and
Ashley wore pale lip gloss instead of her usual shiny pink. The
perfect accompaniment to the dress and hair were the pearls
her grandmother had given her before she passed away two
years ago.

She wore a simple strand around her neck and a tiny cluster
at her ears.

Ashley thought she looked perfect. She just hoped everyone
else did as well and that she could pull off the evening with a
smile.

Across the room, the jazz ensemble played. Waiters circled
the room, offering hors d'oeuvres and a choice of white and red
wines. Two bartenders manned the open bar and in addition
to the appetizers offered by the waiters, there was an elegant
buffet arranged by the far wall.

Lights were strung in the fake potted trees, making the
room look festive and bright. Flickering candles illuminated
centerpieces of fresh flowers on each table.

Ashley had fretted endlessly over all the arrangements until
she was sure she was spouting menu choices in her sleep. She'd
tasted each and every one of the appetizers, wrinkling her
nose at some, loving others. She'd made Pippa accompany her,
though, because Pippa's tastes were more refined. Ashley was
pickier and more apt to turn her nose up at fine cuisine.

Now the moment had arrived and though she kept telling
herself that these people didn't matter to her and that they were
her father's and Devon's associates, she couldn't shake the par-

alyzing fear that she'd make some huge mistake and embarrass herself and her husband in front of everyone.

"Ashley, there you are," Pippa said as she made her way through the growing crowd.

"Oh, my God, I'm so glad you're here," Ashley said. "Thank you for coming. I'm a nervous wreck."

Pippa frowned. "Ash, there's no reason for you to be so worked up over this. It's a party. Loosen up. Have some fun. Let your hair down from that godawful bun."

Ashley let out a shaky laugh. "Easy for you to say. You aren't facing a hundred of your husband's closest business associates."

Pippa rolled her eyes. "Come on, let's go get a drink."

Ashley let Pippa lead her over to the bar but when they got there, Ashley ordered water. Pippa raised an eyebrow and Ashley sighed.

"I have a doctor's appointment tomorrow," Ashley whispered. "Don't you dare say a word to anyone, okay? I haven't told anyone I even suspect I might be pregnant. I took one of those damn home pregnancy tests and it was inconclusive but I haven't had my period yet and I'm sure I'm late. So until I know, I don't want to drink anything."

"What time is your appointment?" Pippa demanded.

"Ten in the morning."

"Okay, then here's what's going to happen. Carly, Tabitha and I are going to wait for you at Oscar's and you're going to come straight over for lunch after your appointment so you can tell us the news one way or another."

Ashley nodded. "Okay. I'll need the support regardless of the outcome. I'm kind of undecided about this whole thing."

Pippa blinked in surprise. "You mean you aren't sure you want to be pregnant?"

"Yes. No. Maybe. I don't know," she said miserably.

"Ash, what the hell is going on with you lately? All you've ever wanted is to have children."

Ashley bit her lip in consternation as she saw Devon making his way toward her. "Look, I can't talk about it now. I'll see you at lunch tomorrow after my appointment. And don't breathe a word! I haven't told anyone. Not even Dev."

Pippa looked at her oddly but went silent as Devon approached.

"There you are," Devon said when he got to the two women. He kissed Pippa's cheek in greeting and then tucked Ashley's hand in his. "If you don't mind, Pippa, I'm going to steal my wife for a bit. There are some people I want her to meet."

Pippa leaned over to kiss Ashley's cheek. "See you tomorrow," she whispered softly. "Take care of yourself."

Ashley smiled her thanks and allowed Devon to lead her away. For the next hour, she smiled and quietly listened as Devon introduced her around and discussed things she had no clue about. But she pretended interest and glued herself to his every word, nodding when she thought it was appropriate.

Her headache had worked itself down her neck until it hurt to even move it. Her cheeks ached from the permanent smile and her feet were killing her.

The old Ashley would have kicked off her shoes, pulled her hair down and found someone to talk with about things she understood. Finding or starting conversation was never difficult for her.

The new Ashley was going to survive this night even if it killed her.

Devon seemed appreciative of her effort. He'd told her she looked beautiful and he'd smiled at her often as he took her from group to group. Maybe she had imagined it or maybe it was wishful thinking on her part but she'd sworn she saw pride reflected in those golden eyes of his.

"Stay right here," Devon said as he parked her on the perimeter of the makeshift dance floor. "I have to find your father. He's announcing his retirement tonight."

She nodded and dutifully stood where he'd left her even

though her feet were about to throb right off her legs and her head hurt so bad her vision was fuzzing.

She was careful to wear a smile and not let her discomfort show. Instead she turned her thoughts to the possibility of her being pregnant.

It was true she'd lived the past week in denial. She hadn't entertained the thought. Hadn't wanted to think about it because if she acknowledged the possibility, then she had to consider the reality of her marriage and whether she was ready to bring a child into such uncertainty.

The previous night with Devon had been... Her smile faltered and she quickly recovered. It had been wonderful. But what was it exactly? Sex? Lust? It couldn't be considered making love. Not when he didn't love her.

He'd been exceedingly tender. She was still embarrassed that she'd lost control of her emotions and cried in front of him. It felt manipulative and she still worried that the only reason he'd had sex with her was because she'd been upset and he wanted to comfort her.

He'd left for work this morning before she'd awakened. She'd overslept—another reason she suspected she was pregnant. She was so tired that some days it was all she could do to remain upright. Twice she'd succumbed to the urge to take a nap simply because she would have lapsed into unconsciousness otherwise.

So she hadn't been able to gauge his mood after they had sex. She had no idea if it changed anything or nothing at all. And she hated the uncertainty. Hated not knowing her place in the world or in this relationship.

Devon had been good to her. He'd been kind. But she didn't want good or kind. She didn't want him to feel sorry for her because he'd broken her heart. She wanted his love.

She could feel the anxiety and rush of anger and confusion crawling over her skin, tightening and heating until the sensation reached her cheeks. She curled and uncurled her fingers at her sides, the only outward reaction she'd allow herself as she sought to calm the turmoil wreaking havoc with her mind.

Maybe it was best she didn't dwell on her possible pregnancy. She was already uptight enough without causing herself full-scale panic.

Her father stepped up onto the elevated platform along with Devon. Ashley's mom stood—just as she always had—by her husband's side. But Devon hadn't wanted Ashley there. He'd wanted her here. All the way across the floor from him. She didn't know if there was any significance to that. Her ego was bruised enough to conjure all sorts of pathetic scenarios that spiked the self-pity meter.

For half an hour her father talked, fondly recounting memories, thanking his staff and his family. She smiled faintly when he singled her out and gave her an indulgent, fatherly smile. Then he went on to say that he was stepping down and that Devon would be succeeding him.

There were surprised murmurs from some. Nods from others who obviously suspected such a thing. A few raised eyebrows but most notably, she noticed that people's gazes found her. There were knowing smiles. A few whispers. Nods in her direction.

Her facade was starting to crack. Her smile was beginning to falter. It was as if the world had put two and two together and said, "Aha! Now we get it."

She just wished she did. She stared around, looking for a possible escape path, but she was surrounded by people. All looking at her. Or between her and Devon. Those damn knowing smiles. The smirks of a few women.

It was the worst night of her entire life. Worse than even her wedding night.

Devon found himself surrounded by a throng of people offering their congratulations. He had only taken one step away from William before everyone had descended. Family members. Staff members. Some offering sincere congratulations. Some clearly wary and uncertain. But that was to be expected. Any time change was announced, fear took hold. It was too early to be offering anyone reassurances. Who knew what would happen over the course of the next few months when a changing of the guard would take place and Devon would be at the helm of what would now be the world's most exclusive line of resorts and luxury hotels.

Tonight, though, Devon was celebrating his own victory of sorts. He'd cornered William before the party had begun and told him that Copeland was going to sponsor Ashley's animal shelter.

William had been opposed until Devon threatened to refuse to take William's place in the company. Devon wanted full sponsorship with a yearly budget allocated to the shelter. He was determined that Ashley wouldn't shed another damn tear over her beloved animals.

His father-in-law grumbled and told Devon he was a besotted fool, but he'd given in, telling Devon he'd just do as he damn well wanted when he took over anyway. Which was absolutely true, but they didn't have that much time and he needed William's cooperation to fund the shelter now so it wouldn't have to close.

Now he just needed the right opportunity to tell Ashley the good news. Tonight in bed after the party seemed perfect. Then he'd make love to her until they were both insensible.

He was yanked from his thoughts when he saw Cam pushing his way through the crowd. He grinned when Cam got to him and he slapped his friend on the back. "Well, we did it. Everything. Copeland. The new resort. Oh, ye of little faith."

Cam ignored Devon's ribbing. His expression was grim and his gaze was focused over Devon's shoulder across the room. "What the hell have you done to her, Dev?"

Devon reared his head back. "Excuse me?" He turned, looking for the source of Cam's attention, but all he saw was

Ashley, standing where he'd left her so she wouldn't be swallowed up by the crowd.

Cam shook his head then turned his gaze on Devon. "You don't even see it, do you?"

Devon's eyes narrowed. "What the hell are you talking about?"

Cam made a sound of disgust. "Look at her, Dev."

Again, Devon followed Cam's gaze to Ashley. He studied her a long moment.

"Really look at her, Dev. Take a long, hard look."

Devon battled a surge of irritation. He was about to tell Cam to go to hell when Ashley rubbed her hand over her forehead. The gesture seemed to make abundantly clear what perhaps he'd missed before. Maybe he'd been missing for a while. Or maybe it just took Cam drawing his attention to it.

She was pale, her face drawn. She looked tired and exceedingly fragile. She looked…different. Not at all like the vivacious, sparkling woman he'd married.

He frowned. "She probably has a headache."

"You're a dumbass," Cam said in disgust.

Before Devon could respond, Cam turned on his heel and walked away, leaving Devon baffled by the anger in his friend's voice.

But he didn't have time to figure out Cam's mood or what bug was up his ass. Ashley looked exhausted. Her forehead was creased in pain and she rubbed the back of her neck. He was more convinced than ever that she had one of her headaches.

He pushed his way through the few people standing between him and where William now stood with his son, Eric.

"I'm going to take Ashley home," he said to William. "Please give our apologies to our guests."

William looked up in concern while Eric frowned and immediately sought Ashley out in the crowd.

"Is something wrong?" William asked.

"Everything's fine," Devon said in an effort to calm the older man. "I think she has a headache."

Eric scowled, his blue eyes flashing as he stared holes through Devon. "She seems to be having headaches quite frequently these days."

Devon wasn't going to stick around to argue the point. He nodded at William and then went to collect Ashley.

He found her conversing with two of the people who worked in the Tricorp offices. Or rather *they* were doing all the conversing. Ashley stood smiling and nodding.

"Excuse us please, gentlemen," Devon said smoothly. "I'd like to steal my wife if you don't mind."

The relief on her face made him wince. She was obviously suffering and she'd had to stand here through her father's speech.

His plans for the evening melted away. His primary concern now was getting her home so he could take care of her. The news about the shelter could wait until tomorrow. They'd have dinner together—another of her experimental concoctions, no doubt—and then he'd tell her that her animals were safe.

He drew her in close, noting again the fatigue etched in her features. But more than that, it was as if the light had been doused from her usually expressive eyes.

He experienced a tightening sensation in his chest but he shook it off and focused his attention on her.

"We're leaving."

She looked up in surprise. "But why? The party will be going on for hours yet."

"You're hurting," he said quietly. "Headache?"

A dull flush worked over her features. "It's okay. I'm fine, really. There's no need for you to leave. I can have Pippa take me home or I can just catch a cab."

"The hell I'll have you leave here in a cab," he bit out. "I've done what I needed to do here. The rest is William's night. I won't have you suffering when you could be at home in bed after taking your medication."

Her shoulders sagged a bit and she nodded her acceptance. He put his hand to her back, noting again just how fragile she felt. It wasn't something he could even describe. How did someone feel fragile? But there was an aura of vulnerability that surrounded her like a fog. He wasn't imagining it.

He guided her toward the door, not stopping to acknowledge the people who spoke as they passed.

She was silent the entire way home. She sat in the darkened interior of the car, eyes closed and so still that he was afraid to move for fear of disturbing her.

Once back at their apartment, he helped her undress and pulled back the covers so she could crawl into bed. He leaned down to kiss her brow as he pulled the sheet up to her chin.

"I'll go get your medication and something to drink."

To his surprise, she shook her head. "No," she said in a low voice. "I don't want it. I hate the way it makes me feel. I just need to sleep. I'll be fine in the morning."

He frowned but didn't want to argue with her. She needed to take the damn medicine. She was obviously in a lot of pain. But her eyes were already closed and her soft breathing signaled that she was relaxing or at least trying to.

"All right," he conceded. "But if you aren't better in the morning, you're taking the medicine."

She nodded without opening her eyes. "Promise."

Seventeen

Devon woke Ashley the next morning long enough to ascertain how she was feeling. Ashley assured him she was fine even though her stomach still churned with humiliation and upset. In truth, she just wanted him gone. The last thing she wanted was a set of eyes on her when she was on the verge of cracking.

After he left for work, she shuffled into the shower and stood for a long time underneath the heated spray. Afterward she didn't linger in the bathroom long. She dried her hair because of the cold, but pulled it back into a ponytail. She was too on edge to worry over makeup and just made do with moisturizer.

She was in turns scared and dismayed over the prospect of pregnancy. At times she firmly hoped she wasn't expecting. Others, she held a secret, ridiculous hope that a pregnancy would… What? She laughed helplessly at just how naive she was. Even as she knew a child would in no way fix a doomed relationship, there was a part of her that wondered if Devon would grow to love the mother of his child.

It angered her that she could even entertain such a notion. Why on earth would she settle for a man loving her because she produced his offspring? If he couldn't love her before that, why would she even care what happened after she popped out a kid?

Unrequited love sucked. There were no two ways about it.

If she had it to do all over again, she'd put a definite "wait and see" on any childbearing. Or at least get through the honeymoon without any life-altering surprises.

She ate a light breakfast to settle her stomach. She couldn't be entirely certain if her queasy morning stomach was due to pregnancy or her rather fragile emotional state of late. Or maybe subconsciously she wanted to be pregnant and so had convinced herself of the possibility. Weren't there women who had false pregnancies?

Her nervousness grew as she got into a cab to go to the doctor's office. The only person who knew what she was doing today was Pippa. And well, now Tabitha and Carly would know as well, but she was counting on them to get her through either scenario. Pregnant or not pregnant.

At the clinic, she filled out the paperwork and waited impatiently for the nurse to call her back. After answering a myriad of questions, she was asked to pee in a cup. They drew blood and then she was asked to wait in the reception area.

For twenty of the longest minutes of her life.

She fidgeted. She flipped through a magazine. Finally she got up to pace as she took in the other women in various stages of pregnancy.

Finally the nurse called her back. Ashley hurried toward the door and was escorted to a private sitting area outside one of the exam rooms.

"Well?" she blurted, unable to remain silent a moment longer.

The nurse smiled. "You're pregnant, Mrs. Carter. Judging by when you say your last period was, I'd say maybe six weeks at most. But we'll schedule a sonogram so we can better determine dates."

Ashley's stomach bottomed out. She broke out in a cold sweat and her head began pounding until her vision was blurred.

"Are you all right?" the nurse asked gently.

Ashley swallowed rapidly and nodded. "I'm fine. Just a little shocked. I mean, I suspected but maybe secretly I didn't really believe I was."

The nurse gave her a sympathetic look. "It takes time to adjust. It can be a little overwhelming at first. The important thing is for you to rest, take it easy. Take a little time to let it sink in. We're doing lab work and will check your HCG levels to make sure they're in an appropriate range. If there's any cause for concern, we'll call you. Otherwise, set up an appointment with the receptionist on your way out for your first visit to the doctor. We'll do your sonogram then."

Ashley walked out of the clinic a little—okay, a lot—numb. Again, it wasn't a huge shock. She and Devon hadn't done anything to prevent pregnancy at all. In fact they'd openly embraced the idea—at her instigation—but now she wondered if he was even as open to the idea as he'd let on. How could she be sure he hadn't said whatever was necessary to get her to agree to marry him?

Her mouth turned down in an unhappy frown as she laid her head back against the seat of the cab. She should have asked the nurse what she could take for a headache now that she was pregnant.

But she doubted even the strongest pain medication would help the roar in her ears and the nerves that were balanced on a razor's edge.

The cab dropped her off half a block from the restaurant where she was meeting her friends and she bundled her coat around her as she pushed through people hurrying by. She ducked into the bright eatery and scanned the small seating area for the girls.

In the corner, Pippa stood up and waved. Tabitha and Carly both turned immediately and motioned her over with a flurry of hands.

Ashley nearly ran, desperate to be surrounded by the comfort of her best friends in the world.

"So?" Pippa demanded before Ashley had even had a chance to shrug out of her coat. "Tell us!"

"Are you pregnant?" Tabitha asked.

Ashley flopped into her chair, wrung out from the events of the past weeks. To her utter horror, tears welled in her eyes. It was like knocking the final stone from an already weakened dam.

Her friends stared at her in shock as she dissolved into tears.

"Oh, my God, Ashley, what's wrong? Honey, it's okay, you have plenty of time to get pregnant," Carly soothed.

Tabitha and Pippa wrapped their arms around her from both sides and hugged her fiercely.

"I *am* pregnant," she said on a sob.

That earned her looks of bewilderment all around. Pippa took charge, taking a table napkin and dabbing at Ashley's tears. Her friends sat quietly, soothing and hugging her until finally she got her sobs under control and they diminished to quiet sniffles.

"What the hell is going on?" Pippa asked bluntly. "You look like hell, Ash. And you haven't been yourself. What the hell was that last night with the weird hair and the dress you wouldn't normally get caught dead in?"

"Pippa!" Tabitha scolded. "Can't you see how upset she is?"

"She's right," Carly said in a grim voice. "Besides we're her friends and we love her. We can get away with telling her she looks like crap."

Tabitha sighed. "I think what they're delicately trying to say is you just don't look happy, Ash. We're worried about you."

"Everything's such a mess," Ashley said as tears welled up all over again.

"We've got all day," Pippa said firmly. "Now tell us what's going on with you."

The entire story came spilling out. Every humiliating detail, right down to the disaster of a wedding night and her decision to make Devon fall in love with her.

The three women looked stunned. Then anger fired in Pippa's eyes. "That son of a bitch! I hate him!"

"So do I," Tabitha announced.

"I'd like to kick him right between the legs," Carly muttered.

"You aren't going to stand for this are you?" Pippa demanded.

"I don't know what to do," Ashley said wearily.

Carly grabbed Ashley's hands. "Look at me, honey. You are a beautiful, loving, generous woman. You are perfect just like you are. The only one who needs to change in this relationship is that jerk you married. I'm so pissed right now I can't even see straight. I cannot believe his nerve. I wouldn't change a single thing about you and moreover he doesn't deserve you."

"Amen," Pippa growled. "You need to tell him to take a long walk off the short end of a pier."

Tabitha pulled Ashley into her arms and hugged her tightly. Then she pulled away and gently wiped at the tears on Ashley's cheeks.

"No one who truly loves you should ever want you to change. And no one who wants to change that essential part that makes you *you* deserves a single moment of your time."

"I love you guys," Ashley said brokenly. "You can't even imagine how much I needed you right now."

"I just wish you'd confided in us sooner," Pippa said. "Nobody should have to endure all of what you've endured alone. That's what friends are for. We love you. We would have kicked his sorry ass weeks ago if we'd known."

Ashley cracked a watery smile. "What would I do without you all?"

"Let's not even consider the possibility since you're never going to be without us," Carly said.

"So what are you going to do, hon?" Tabitha asked, her voice full of concern.

Ashley took a deep breath because until right now, at this very moment, she hadn't known. Or maybe she had but had pushed it aside, unwilling to accept the decision that her heart had already made.

"I'm going to tell him I can't do this," she said softly.

"Good for you," Pippa said fiercely.

"You're leaving him?" Carly asked.

Ashley sighed again. "I can't stay with him. I deserve better. I deserve a man who loves me and doesn't want to change me. I'm tired of trying to be someone I'm not. I liked myself the way I was. I don't like this person I've become."

"That a girl," Tabitha said. "And don't you worry even for a minute about the baby. You have us. You know your parents will support you. We'll be with you every step of the way. We'll babysit. We'll go to the doctor with you. We'll even coach you in the delivery room."

"Oh God, stop before you make me cry again," Ashley choked out.

"Do you want one of us to go with you?" Carly asked anxiously. "I don't want you to have to do this alone. Pippa would be awesome to take with you. She can be scary when people mess with someone she loves."

Pippa grinned.

"No," Ashley said, squaring her shoulders. "This is something I have to do on my own. It's time I regained control over my own life and future. I haven't had it since Devon walked into my life."

"I'm so proud of you, Ash," Tabitha said.

"We all are," Pippa said firmly. "If you need a place to stay until you get everything sorted out, any one of us will be more than happy to let you stay as long as you need."

Ashley looked at her three friends and some of the terrible ache in her chest dissolved at the love and loyalty she saw burning in their eyes. She really would be okay. Things would suck for a while, but she was going to be okay. She'd get through this. She had family and friends—the very best of friends—and now she had a child to focus on.

The moment the nurse had confirmed that she had a life growing inside her, Ashley's entire world had changed. Her priorities had shifted and she'd instantly known that she had to do what was best for her and her child.

It had been a powerful moment of realization.

Calm settled over her. Oh, she was still terrified—and heartbroken. That wouldn't change overnight. But now she knew what she had to do and she couldn't escape the inevitability of the path that for once *she* had chosen instead of it choosing her.

Eighteen

Devon was having a hard time concentrating. He'd already blown three phone calls. He'd sent an email to the wrong recipient and replied to another thinking it was someone else. His focus was completely and utterly shot and he couldn't even pinpoint exactly what had him so out of sorts.

He was concerned for Ashley, definitely. He hadn't wanted to leave her that morning, but she'd insisted she was fine and that he should go into work. Still, he had a nagging sensation tugging at his chest that wouldn't go away.

Something just wasn't right.

He picked up his phone to call Ashley's cell but was interrupted by his door opening. He looked up and frowned. His secretary hadn't announced a visitor and he knew damn well he didn't have an appointment now.

To his surprise, Eric Copeland strode into the room, his expression grim. He stopped in front of Devon's desk and planted his palms down on the polished wood.

"What the hell have you done to my sister?"

Devon pushed back and shot up out of his chair. "What the hell are you talking about? I'm getting damn tired of people asking me what I've done to her. If you're asking why we left the party last night, she had a headache and I didn't want her to suffer needlessly. I took her home and put her to bed."

Eric made a sound of disgust. "You may not know this about Ashley but the only time she gets these headaches with any frequency is when she's stressed or unhappy. I find it pretty telling that she returned from her honeymoon after only two days because of a headache and that since then, she's suffered them on a regular basis."

It was a fist to Devon's gut. He sank back into his chair as Eric stood seething over him.

"My sister looks desperately unhappy," Eric continued. "I don't know what the hell is going on, but I don't like what I see. She's changed and something tells me you have everything to do with that."

"Maybe she's finally growing up," Devon said tightly. "Her family hasn't done her any favors by coddling her and shielding her from the world around her."

Eric gave him a look of pure disgust. The cold fury emanating from the younger man slapped Devon squarely in the face. It pricked at Devon and aroused an instinctive need to defend himself. The idea that his marriage was being picked apart by this outsider roused his ire even as a voice in the back of his mind whispered to him to listen.

"Her family loves her just like she is," Eric bit out. "She is cherished and adored by us all. She is appreciated for the beautiful, warm, loving person she is and we'd damn well never try to change her. Anyone that would doesn't *deserve* her."

He spun around and stalked toward the door but then he stopped and turned back to Devon, his lips curled into a snarl. "I don't know what the hell kind of deal you struck with my father but he was wrong. Dead wrong. You weren't the right man for my sister. The right man would know and appreciate what a gift he'd been given. I'm putting you on notice right now. I'm watching you. If Ashley isn't more herself in very short order, I'm coming after you with everything I've got. I hadn't planned to take over the business for my father, but if the choices are having you as a part of the family and making my sister miserable or me sucking it up and taking over myself, I'll do it."

Devon's lips thinned but he acknowledged Eric's ultimatum with a tight nod.

With another dark look, Eric stalked out of the door.

Devon stared out his window in brooding silence after Eric's abrupt departure. Then he stared down at his phone, suddenly afraid to make the call he'd planned just minutes before.

It also occurred to him that she hadn't called him at work in weeks. Not once. No more silly Tinker Bell chimes that amused his coworkers to no end. Not even a mushy text message like she'd done so often before.

He hadn't given it much thought. Things had been so busy after the wedding, with William wanting to move into retirement and the new resort going up, as well as the endless planning sessions for the future.

He'd honestly just forged ahead, hoping that with time, Ashley would get over her initial upset and see that things really hadn't changed that much between them. But a sick feeling settled into his stomach as he realized—truly realized—that everything had changed. And most notably, *she* had changed.

A ping sounded, signaling the intercom, and Devon raised his head irritably. Now his secretary wanted to talk to him? Giving him a heads-up on Eric's arrival would have been nice. But he forgot all about his irritation when he heard what she had to say.

"Mr. Carter, your wife is here to see you."

Adrenaline surged in his veins.

"Send her in," Devon demanded, rising from his seat.

Ashley hadn't ever set foot in his office. Not even when they were dating. She'd called him. Texted him. Sent him sweet emails. But she'd never actually come into his building.

He was striding across the room, fully intending to meet her, when the door opened and she hesitantly walked in. He stopped abruptly, taken aback by the starkness of her features. She was pale, her face was drawn and her eyes were heavy and dull.

An uneasy feeling crept up his spine as she stared back at him.

"Are you busy?" she asked in a soft voice. "Have I come at a bad time?"

"Of course not. Come, have a seat. Would you like something to drink?"

He was suddenly nervous and he hated that feeling. Somehow she'd managed to completely upend his confidence. Much like she'd upended his life.

She shook her head but took a seat on the small sofa in the small sitting area of his office. "I needed to talk to you, Devon."

It was only natural that any man hearing those words from his wife would dread what followed. But coming from Ashley, they seemed so…final.

"All right," he said quietly. He took a seat across from her and studied the tiredness in her eyes. Those rich, vibrant eyes looked…bleak. Without hope. That was what he'd been reaching for. What had eluded him about the way she looked. He caught his breath, suddenly filled with an impending sense of doom. She looked…hopeless, and Ashley was nothing if not eternally optimistic. Had he ever considered such a thing a flaw? He was ashamed to say he had. Now he just wanted it back.

"I'm pregnant," she said baldly. There was no emotion. No

accompanying excitement. No flash of joy. Frankly, he was bewildered by her reaction.

"That's wonderful," he said huskily.

But her expression said it was anything but wonderful. She looked as though she was battling tears.

"I can't do this anymore," she said in a choked voice.

Alarm blistered up his spine and rammed into the base of his skull. "What do you mean?"

She rose and it was all he could do not to tie her to the damn sofa because he had a sudden sense that she was slipping away from him in more ways than one.

Her hands shook but she exerted admirable control over her emotions as she courageously faced him down.

"This marriage. You asked how long it would take to determine whether it would work. The truth is, it was never going to work. It's taken me this long to realize it, but I deserve more. We both do. You deserve to find a woman you can love and that you won't be manipulated into marrying. I deserve a man who adores me and wants to be married to me. Someone who won't try to change me. Someone who accepts me, faults and all. Someone who loves flighty, impulsive Ashley and isn't embarrassed by her."

Tears clouded her eyes and her voice grew thick with emotion. "I thought… I thought I could make you love me, Dev. It was a mistake from the beginning to even try. It was a hard lesson for me to learn but I can't be someone I'm not even if it meant you'd eventually love the new me. Because it wouldn't be Ashley you loved. It would be someone I made up and all the while the real Ashley would be standing there, unloved. I can't do that to myself. And I can't do it to my child. I want to be a woman and a mother I can be proud of first. Before anyone else. I have to love and be at peace with myself, and you know what? I am. I liked me just fine. Was I perfect? No, but I was happy in my own skin and my family and friends accept that person. Someday there'll be a man who'll accept

me, too. Until then, I'd rather be alone and true to myself than
with someone who places conditions on his ability to love and
accept me."

So stunned was he by her declaration that he stood while
she walked quietly toward the door. When he realized she'd
already slipped by him, he whirled around, calling her name,
the lump in his throat so huge that it came out as a mere croak.

But the door had already closed quietly behind her, leaving
him standing there so numb...and broken.

Dread consumed him. The realization, the true realization
of just what he'd done threatened to completely unravel him.
Oh, God. What had he done?

His legs buckled and would no longer sustain his weight.
He staggered back onto the couch and slumped forward, burying his face in his hands.

She was right and so very wrong all at the same time. The
realization was as clear to him as if someone had hit him over
the head with it.

He'd destroyed something infinitely precious and he'd never
forgive himself for it. He didn't deserve forgiveness.

Dear God, was this what he'd done to her? She'd come into
his office and delivered the news of her pregnancy in a dis-
passionate fashion, as if she were telling him that she had a
dentist appointment or that she was buying new shoes.

Where she'd once jumped up and down and squealed her
joy over her cousin's pregnancy and vowed she'd do the same
over her own pregnancy, she'd related the news with dead eyes
and a broken spirit.

He'd done that to her. No one else. Him and his high-
handed, arrogant opinions of how she should act or not act.
He'd taken something beautiful and precious and had spit on
it.

He'd suffocated a ray of sunshine and sucked every bit of
joy and life from her.

Cam was right. Eric was right. Ashley was right. He didn't

deserve her. They'd seen clearly what he'd blithely ignored. In his arrogance, he'd assumed he was right and that he knew what was best for Ashley.

He had tried to change her. And she was bloody perfect just as she was. He hadn't even realized how much he'd missed all the things he professed to be annoyed over. The random calls at work just to say she loved him. The sudden attacks of affection when she'd throw her arms around him. Her exuberance around others.

She hadn't cleaned and organized their apartment because she felt like it. She'd eradicated every hint of her presence there because she'd thought that's what he wanted. She'd tried to become this image of the perfect wife to please him. He himself had thought he wanted her to.

The cooking. The endless trying to kill herself to please him. She'd gone from a vibrant breath of fresh air to a subdued, beaten-down shadow of her former self.

She no longer sparkled. All because he was the biggest ass on the face of the planet.

His pulse ratcheted up and the sick feeling inside him grew as he realized just how long it had been since she'd said she loved him. Since she'd demonstrated any outward affection for him. Since she'd simply smiled and seemed happy.

Tears burned his eyelids. He'd taken something so very beautiful and he'd crushed it. He'd rejected her love. The very gift of herself. He'd arrogantly told her in essence that she wasn't good enough for him. That he knew better. That she wasn't worthy of him.

A low moan escaped him. Not good enough for him? He wasn't good enough to lick her boots.

In clear and startling detail, he realized what perhaps he'd fought from the very first moment he laid eyes on Ashley. He loved her. Not the new, subdued Ashley. He loved the impulsive, passionate, sparkly Ashley. And the very thing he loved the most was what he'd tried to kill.

Rafe and Ryan had nothing on him when it came to being complete and utter bastards to the women who loved them. Devon had surpassed any amount of sin a man committed against someone they claimed to care for.

How could he possibly expect Ashley to forgive him when he'd never be able to forgive himself?

She was pregnant with his child and she was leaving him.

He didn't deserve her. He should let her walk away and find someone who adored her beyond reason and would never ever treat her as he had.

But he couldn't do it. He couldn't be that selfless. *He* adored her beyond reason and if it took the rest of his damn life, he would make it up to her for every wrong he'd done to her.

But first he had to make damn sure she didn't walk out of his life forever.

Nineteen

Ashley tugged the coat tighter around her as she stepped from the cab in front of her parents' apartment building. She had no desire to face them today but she needed to get it over with and she wanted the comfort only her mother could provide.

Devon had already called her cell a dozen times until finally she'd shut it off so it would stop ringing. She'd expected resistance. She was fortunate that she'd caught him off guard enough that she'd been able to get out of his office without much fuss.

But now he would want to talk to her. No doubt he'd give her another lecture about being impulsive and reckless and whatever other adjectives he'd want to assign to her. Then he'd inform her that there was no reason they couldn't have an enjoyable marriage, blah blah blah.

She wanted more than some damn enjoyable marriage. She wanted…awesome. She wanted a man who loved her and celebrated her for who she was. Maybe she'd never have it. But she damn sure wasn't going to settle for someone her father had bribed to marry her.

Which was another reason she'd come to her parents' apartment. Because first she was going to tell her father to stop interfering in her life. Then she wanted a hug from her mother.

She walked into the apartment and took off her coat. "Mom?" she called. "Daddy?"

Gloria Copeland hurried out of the kitchen and smiled her welcome. "Hi, darling. What brings you over today? I wish you'd called. I would have made sure I had tea ready."

"Where's Daddy?" Ashley asked quietly. "I need to talk to him. To you both, actually."

Gloria frowned. "I'll go get him. Is something wrong?"

"You could say that."

Alarm flashed across her mother's face. "Go sit down in the living room. We'll be right there."

Her mom hurried away and Ashley made her way into the spacious living room. Instead of sitting, she went to the fireplace, grateful for the warmth. She was cold on the inside and it felt as though she'd never be warm again.

A moment later, she heard the footsteps of her parents and she turned slowly to face them.

"Ashley, baby, what's wrong?" her father asked sharply.

Both her mother and her father stood a short distance away, impatient and worried. She drew a deep breath and took the plunge. "I've left Devon and I'm pregnant."

Gloria gasped and put her hand to her mouth. William's eyes narrowed and he frowned. "What the hell happened?"

"*You* happened," she said bitterly. "How could you, Daddy? How could you manipulate us both that way?"

Her father threw up his arm in anger and swore. "Damn it, I told him not to tell you."

"He didn't. I found out on my wedding night. Can you possibly imagine how awful it was to find out on my wedding night that my father had all but bought and paid for my husband?"

"William, what on earth is she talking about?" Gloria asked in bewilderment.

It relieved Ashley that at least her mother hadn't known. She wouldn't have been able to handle the double deception.

"He made me part of the Tricorp deal," Ashley said with more calm than she felt. "He forced Devon to marry me or the deal was off the table."

"Damn it, it wasn't like that," her father bit out. "You make it sound like…" He dragged a hand through his hair and closed his eyes wearily. "I just wanted what was best for you. I thought Devon would take care of you. He seemed perfect for you."

"I can take care of myself. I don't need a man to do that. I want a man who wants me for who I am, not because my father waves a lucrative deal in front of him. I want someone who *loves* me."

"Oh darling," Gloria said, finally finding her voice. She rushed forward and enfolded Ashley in her arms. "I'm so very sorry. How awful for you. I had no idea."

Ashley closed her eyes, absorbing the love and acceptance she'd been denied with Devon.

Her mom pulled away and gently stroked a hand through Ashley's hair. "What about you being pregnant? When did you find out?"

"I went to the doctor this morning. Then I went to see Devon."

"Ashley, are you sure about this?" William asked. "I don't believe for a moment that Devon doesn't care about you. Think about what you're doing here, honey. Do you really want to throw everything away because of the way you met? I understand your anger and I take full responsibility. Devon never wanted to deceive you. It was me from the start."

She had to take a moment as she battled tears. "He doesn't like the real me. He thinks I'm flighty, irresponsible, impulsive, too trusting. He wants to change everything about me.

How can you possibly think this is a man I'd want to be with? Is that really who you'd want your daughter married to? What would that teach my daughter if I stay with a man who doesn't value me? How can I expect her to have any self-respect if her mother doesn't?"

Her mother wrapped an arm around her shoulders and glared her husband down with furious eyes. "I can't believe you did this, William. What in the hell were you thinking? You may as well have told your daughter that she doesn't matter. You've pulled some stupid stunts in your time, but this takes the cake."

William sighed. "Ashley, please don't be angry with me. I only wanted the best for you. You're my only daughter and I just wanted to see your future secured. I thought that you and Devon would make a sound match. I was wrong and I'm sorrier than you can possibly imagine."

"You aren't pulling the plug on this deal," Ashley said in a low voice. "You won't punish Devon because he can't love me. If you think he's the best choice for the business then leave me out of it. I'd appreciate being able to make my own choices in the future, free of manipulation."

"I do love you, baby. Please believe that. I never meant to hurt you. Devon tried to tell me but I wouldn't listen. I thought I knew better. He wanted me to tell you everything. He didn't want to deceive you but I tied his hands and for that I'm sorry."

Tears welled in her eyes. Who knew what may have happened if they'd just been left alone?

William hesitantly pulled her into his arms and hugged her tight. "You know you can count on me and your mother to help you with whatever you need, and we'll be here for the baby when it comes."

"I know," she whispered. "And I love you too, Daddy. Just let me make my own mistakes from now on. Your heart was in the right place but now I've fallen in love with a man who can never love the real me."

He slowly released her and her mom pulled her into another hug. "Do you want me to send someone over for your things? You know you can stay here as long as you like."

Ashley shook her head. "I'm going to stay with Pippa for a bit until I figure out what my next step is. I need to find a better job. I have a child to consider now. Devon is right about one thing. It's time to pull my head out of the clouds and grow up."

How long could she possibly avoid him? Devon paced his office, though he hadn't gotten any work done in the three days since Ashley had walked out on him. He hadn't slept. He'd worn out his phone trying to call her. He'd called her friends, her parents, every family member he had a number for.

The reception had been understandably chilly.

He didn't care. He had no pride where Ashley was concerned. He didn't care if he came across as the most pathetic, lovesick guy who'd ever lived. He just wanted her back. He wanted her stuff strewn all over his apartment. He wanted to be able to smell her as soon as he walked into a room. He wanted her to be happy again. He wanted her to smile.

When he wasn't at the office, he was at the apartment, waiting. She hadn't returned. Not even to get her things. All her clothes were still neatly hung in the closet. Her shoes—and there were a ton of shoes—were stacked in boxes on the shelves in his closet. Ashley never went anywhere without her shoes and the fact that she still hadn't returned to the apartment worried him.

If only she'd answer her damn phone. Or one of the hundreds of texts he'd sent her. He just wanted to know she was all right. Worry was eating a hole in his gut. She was pregnant. What if she had another one of her headaches? Who would take care of her?

Eric had said she had frequent headaches when she was unhappy. Devon had made her miserable. Her medication was also at the apartment but surely she couldn't take it now that she was pregnant. He could at least hold her, rub her head, make sure it was cool and dark in the room.

If she would just talk to him. Just give him a chance to tell her how much he loved her. He hadn't realized how much he missed the sunshine she brought into his life until it was gone. Snuffed out over careless, thoughtless words he'd thrown at her.

His cell rang and he scrambled for it, nearly dropping it in his haste to see if it was Ashley calling. Disappointment nearly flattened him when he saw it was Rafael. With a heavy sigh, he put the phone to his ear and muttered a low hello.

"It's a girl!" Rafael said in a jubilant voice. "A beautiful six-pound, twelve-ounce baby girl. She was born an hour ago."

Devon's eyes closed and he swallowed back the bitter disappointment. He was so envious of his friend in this moment that it took everything he had not to throw the phone at the wall.

"Hey man, that's great. How is Bryony doing?"

"Oh she's wonderful. What a trooper. I'm so damn proud of her. She breezed right through labor. I think she was a hell of a lot stronger than I was. I was ready to fall over by the time the little one made her appearance. But boy, is she gorgeous. Looks just like her mama."

Devon could practically hear Rafael beaming through the phone.

"Give her my love," Devon said. "I'm happy for both of you."

"Is everything okay, Dev? You sound like hell if you don't mind me saying."

Devon hesitated. He didn't want to dump on Rafael on the day his daughter was born, but he was at the end of his rope and he could use any advice he could get.

"No," he said bluntly. "Ashley's pregnant and she left me."

"Whoa. Back up a minute. Holy crap. I thought she was

head over heels in love with you? What the hell happened? And damn, you move fast. How far along is she?"

"I have no idea," Devon said in a weary voice. "I don't know anything. She came to my office three days ago, told me she was pregnant and then announced she was leaving me."

"Ouch. That blows, man. I'm sorry to hear it. Is there anything I can do?"

Devon sank into his chair and rotated around so he could watch the falling snow through the window. "Yeah, you can give me some advice. I have to get her back, Rafe."

There was a prolonged silence. Then Rafael blew out his breath. "Okay, well the first question. Do you love her? Or is this more of a 'you're not leaving me because you're pregnant and we should stay married' type thing?"

Devon swore. "I love her. I screwed up but I love her. Not that she'll ever believe me. I messed up so bad with her, Rafe. I make you and Ryan look like choirboys."

"Oh boy. That's bad. That's really, really bad."

"Tell me about it."

"Well, I'll tell you like a certain gentleman once told me when I was standing around with my thumb up my ass wondering how the hell I was going to get Bryony to forgive me. Either go big or go home."

"What the hell is that supposed to mean?"

"It means you need to pull out the big guns. Do something huge. Make a gesture she can't possibly misunderstand. And then get on your knees and grovel. Trust me. The first time on your knees sucks, but if she takes you back, you'll spend the rest of your life on them anyway so better get used to it now."

"If she'll take me back, I'll gladly stay on them," Devon muttered.

"It pains me that I can't even give you hell about falling hard like the rest of us poor schmucks you liked to rag on. You're too pathetic to pick on right now."

"Gee thanks," Devon said dryly. "Don't you have a daughter to go take care of? She probably needs a diaper change or something."

"She's sleeping with her mama, but yeah, I'm going to get back to my family. It's the best feeling in the whole world, Dev. Get your ass out there and get your family back where they belong."

"I will. And thanks, Rafe."

"Hey, no problem, man. Anytime."

Devon slid the phone back into his pocket and pondered his friend's advice. Go big or go home. Pretty solid advice. Now he just had to figure out how big to go. There was absolutely nothing he wouldn't do to convince Ashley to give him another chance.

Twenty

Ashley sat on Pippa's couch, curled underneath a blanket as she sipped hot tea and watched it snow. It had snowed for the last two days, leaving a heavy blanket over the city. She longed for the comfort of her own apartment...or rather Devon's apartment. She bleakly considered that it had never really been her home. But she missed it all the same. Nights like tonight she and Devon would have snuggled in front of the fire and watched a movie.

"Hey, chickie," Pippa said as she settled down the couch from Ash with a bounce. "How are you feeling? Nausea still a problem?"

It was probably the pregnancy hormones—that was what she was blaming anyway—but she got positively weepy over how protective and caring Pippa had been ever since Ashley had moved in. Or sort of moved in, since Ashley hadn't yet worked up the nerve to get her things from Devon's apartment. Instead she'd been borrowing clothes from Pippa. But soon—as in tomorrow—she was going to have to brave going.

"Yes and no. I honestly don't know if it's the pregnancy or the fact I'm upset. I've been so queasy and nothing sounds good. Even my favorite foods have suddenly lost their appeal."

"I'm sure neither is helping," Pippa said dryly. She hesitated a moment as if deciding whether or not to say what was obviously on her mind. But Pippa wasn't one to hold back. "Have you talked to Devon yet, Ash?"

Ashley put her cup down and sighed. "No. I'm a horrible coward."

"No, you aren't," Pippa said fiercely. "It took guts to go to his office and lay it out to him like you did. I'm so freaking proud of you. I so want to be you when I grow up."

Ashley's eyes got all watery again. "Oh my God. I've got to stop this," she said, sniffling back the tears. "Pippa, you're the most put-together person I know. You've got it all. You're smart. You can cook like a dream. You're gorgeous. And you're the best friend I could possibly hope for."

"And strangely I'm still single," Pippa drawled.

Ashley giggled. "Only because you're a picky bitch, as you should be. I could use some lessons from you."

Pippa shifted forward on the couch, her expression suddenly serious. "Ashley, you have no idea how truly special you are. When the rest of us were struggling to find ourselves, sleeping around and experimenting with all the wrong guys, you were so calm and centered. You knew exactly who you were and what you wanted. You've always known who you were. You valued yourself and you refused to settle for less. Just because Devon turned out to be a prick who tried to change you doesn't mean you did anything wrong. You may have lost your way for a very short time, but ultimately you didn't let him change you."

Ashley smiled but inside she wondered if Pippa was right. Devon had changed her. Irrevocably. No matter that she'd resisted and refused to become someone she didn't like, she'd never truly be who she was before Devon entered her life.

But maybe that was what life was all about. People and circumstances changed you. It was what you did with that change that mattered.

The door buzzer sounded and Pippa made a face. "I swear if that's another salesman I'm going to wet down my steps so they'll freeze and anyone coming up will bust their ass. We've had two already this week."

"Are you expecting a delivery? Maybe it's your groceries."

Pippa grew thoughtful. "No, I'm pretty sure I arranged it for tomorrow. But maybe you're right. I'll be right back."

"You sit," Ashley said as she pushed the blanket back. "You've been on your feet all morning. I've done nothing but sit around and feel sorry for myself."

Pippa rolled her eyes but flopped back on the couch as Ashley padded toward the door. Ashley grinned as she imagined Pippa watering down her steps so they'd become icy. It was something she'd totally do.

She opened the door to the street-level apartment and blinked in shock to see Devon standing on the stoop, snow landing on his hair and wetting it. He wore a coat but had no scarf or cap, and he looked like he hadn't slept in a week.

"Hello, Ash," he said in a quiet, determined voice.

She gripped the door until her fingers went numb. "Uh, hi. What are you doing here?"

He laughed. It was a dry, brittle sound that in no way conveyed true amusement. "I haven't seen my wife in a week. She won't return my phone calls or texts. I have no idea if she's okay or where she's staying and she asks me what I'm doing here when I finally track her down."

She swallowed nervously but she held her ground. It was mean-spirited to make him stand out in the cold, but she didn't want him to come in.

"I was going to come by tomorrow to pick up my things," she said in a low voice that barely managed to hide the tremble. "If that's all right with you."

"No, it's not all right with me," he bit out.

Her eyes widened and she took a step back at the vehemence in his voice.

"Can we go somewhere and talk, Ash?"

She shook her head automatically. "I don't think that's a good idea."

His lips formed a grim line. "You don't think it's a good idea. You're pregnant with my child. We're married. We've only been married a short time. And you don't think we have anything to talk about?"

She closed her eyes and put a hand to her forehead in an automatic gesture.

"Ash? Is everything okay?" Pippa called. Then she came up behind Ashley. "Who is it?"

Ashley turned. "It's okay, Pip. It's Devon."

Pippa's expression darkened, but Ashley held up her hand. Pippa reluctantly turned to go back to the living room but she called back in a low voice, "I'll be right here if you need me."

Ashley returned her attention to Devon. "I know we need to talk. I just don't think I'm up to it right now. This has been hard for me, Dev. I don't expect you to believe that, but this isn't easy."

His expression softened and he took a step forward, snow dusting off his hair as he moved. "I know it's not, baby. Please. There's so much I need to say to you. There are things I need to show you. But I can't do that if you won't talk to me. Give me this afternoon. Please. If you still don't want anything to do with me, I'll take you over to the apartment myself and I'll help you pack your things."

She stared back at him, utterly befuddled by the pleading in his voice. He almost looked as though he were holding his breath. And his eyes. They looked...bleak.

"I—I need to get my coat," she said lamely.

The relief that poured over his face was stunning. His eyes

lightened and he immediately straightened, hope flashing in those golden depths.

"And shoes," he said. "I brought some from the apartment. I wasn't sure you had any you loved here."

She gaped at him. "You brought my shoes?"

He shifted uncomfortably. "Six pairs. They're in the trunk of the car. I chose those I thought would be warm and would protect your feet from getting wet in the snow."

Something loosened in her heart and began to slowly unwind.

"That would be great," she said softly. "Let me go get my coat and my cap. If you brought a pair of boots, that would be perfect."

"I'll be right back. Wait here. I don't want you falling on the ice," he said.

He turned and sprinted back toward the street, where his car was parked. She stood there a moment, staring in bemusement as he popped the trunk and bent over to rummage in the boxes.

He rarely drove his own car. She'd only seen the vehicle once. They always used his car service or hailed cabs.

Realizing she was still standing in the wide open doorway, allowing the bitter chill inside, she hastily withdrew into the apartment and shut the door.

She hurried back into the living room, grabbed a brush from the end table and began pulling it through her hair in short, rapid strokes.

"Ash? What's going on?" Pippa asked cautiously.

Ashley stopped and frowned. "I'm not altogether certain. Devon wants to talk. Asked if I'd give him the afternoon and then he'd take me to the apartment and help me pack if that's what I wanted. He's acting…weird."

Pippa snorted. "Of course he is. You dumped him after telling him you were pregnant with his baby. That has a way of altering your priorities."

"I guess I'll go…talk," Ashley said as she put the brush aside.

"Call me later," Pippa said. "I'll want a full report."

Ashley blew Pippa a kiss and went to the closet to retrieve her coat and scarf. She pulled on a cap and tucked her hair carefully underneath before heading back to the door.

When she opened it, Devon was standing there holding a pair of fur-lined boots. When she would have reached for them, he bent over and said, "Here, let me."

She put a hand on his shoulder to balance herself and stood on one foot while he pulled her boot on the other. After he zipped it up, she switched feet and he put the other one on for her.

When he was done, he straightened to his full height and then took her hand to help her down the steps. He walked her to the car and settled her into the passenger seat.

"Where are we going?" she asked as he pulled away into traffic.

"You'll see."

She wrinkled her nose and sighed. He slid his hand over the center console and tangled his fingers with hers.

"Trust me, Ash. I know it's a big thing to ask and I totally don't have the right to ask it of you, but trust me just this once."

The utter sincerity in his voice swayed her as nothing else could. There was raw vulnerability echoed in his every word and expression. He looked as terrible as she felt, almost as if he'd suffered as much as she had.

It didn't make sense to her. She had no doubt that he wasn't exactly celebrating her departure from the marriage, but with the deal still intact, he was getting precisely what he wanted without the unnecessary burden of a wife.

When they pulled up outside the shelter, Ashley sat there, bewildered. "Why are we here, Dev?"

Devon opened his door, walked around to hers and held out his hand. "Come on. There's something I want you to see."

She allowed him to help her out of the car and they hurried toward the entrance of the older building. As soon as they ducked inside, the sounds and smells of the animals filled her senses. Her heart softened when she saw Harry the cat sound asleep on the reception desk. He was their unofficial mascot and the children who often filtered through the shelter in search of a pet loved to pet him as much as he loved being petted.

To her further surprise, Devon ushered her past the reception area and through the hallway lined with cages. He'd never been here before. How could he possibly know where he was going?

He stopped outside the larger room they used for animal orientation when they'd put pet and new owner together for a period of adjustment before the animal was released to his new home.

He gave her a quick, nervous smile and then pushed the door open. Inside, Molly and the other shelter volunteers stood beaming in a line, and when Devon and Ashley walked fully through the entrance, they let out a loud cheer.

"What's going on?" Ashley asked in bewilderment.

"Say hello to your new staff," he said. "You are now the acting director of the Copeland Animal Shelter."

Ashley's eyes went wide as she stared at Molly and then at the other grinning volunteers. Then she glanced back at Devon. "I don't understand. We aren't closing?"

Molly rushed forward and threw her arms around Ashley. "No, we aren't closing! Thanks to your husband. He gave us the funding we needed to stay running. Not only can we stay open, but we also have the money for improvements and for marketing so we can heighten awareness for the animals we need homes for."

She disentangled herself from Molly's embrace and then turned back to Devon. "You did this for me?"

"I did it before you left," he said gruffly. "I talked to your father about it the night of the party. I threatened to refuse to take his position if he didn't agree to fund the shelter."

Her mouth fell open in shock. She wanted to throw her arms around him so badly, but she knew it wouldn't be what he wanted. But he looked so nervous, as if he worried she wouldn't appreciate what he'd done. How could she not?

"I know how much the animals mean to you, Ash."

Tears blurred her vision and her heart ached. She loved him so much. "Thank you," she whispered. "I can never thank you enough for this. It means the world to me."

"You mean the world to me," he said softly.

Her eyes widened and her heart thumped so hard against her chest that she put a hand over her breast to steady herself.

But before she could question him, he turned to the others and said, "As much as we'd love to stay and celebrate with you, I have to take Ashley one more place."

After saying their goodbyes, Devon ushered Ashley out to the car again. She sat in her seat, bemused and a little hopeful, but for what she wasn't sure. Something was different about Devon. Something that went deeper than simple regret or guilt.

"What did you mean, Dev?" she asked softly as they drove away. "Back there when you said I meant the world to you?"

His hands tightened around the steering wheel and his jaw worked up and down.

"Exactly what I said, Ash. There is so much I need to say to you, but I'm asking you to be patient with me. This isn't a conversation I want to have in a car when I'm driving and I can't look at you or touch you. So I'm asking you to give me a little while. There's a place I want to take you and then I want us to talk and I want you to listen to everything I have to say."

Her mouth went dry at the intensity in his voice. He was tense. Almost as if he feared she'd refuse and demand he take her back. Wanting in some way to alleviate his obvious stress, she reached over to lay her hand on his leg.

"Okay, Dev. I'll listen."

Twenty-One

Devon continuously had to ease up on the accelerator as he headed out of the city. He was impatient and time was running out for him, but the roads were slick and the very last thing he wanted to do was endanger his wife and child.

His wife and child.

The words and the image were powerful. *His* wife and child. The woman he loved and had hurt so terribly. A child resting inside her womb. Their creation. His family. Something that belonged solely to him.

What would he do if he wasn't granted a second chance to make amends?

He couldn't—wouldn't—focus on that possibility. To do so would drive him insane. It was up to him to make her forgive him or at least agree to give him one more chance to make it all right.

She was so beautiful, but there was an aura of sadness that surrounded her. It was as if a light had been extinguished or a black cloud had crawled across the sun and clung stubbornly as the storms rolled in.

He wanted her to smile again. He wanted her to be happy. But more than anything he wanted to be *why* she was happy. He wanted her to be happy with *him*.

The trip to Greenwich, Connecticut, took longer than he'd like. The drive was silent and tense. They both seemed nervous and ill at ease. By the time he turned onto road that would wind around to the front of the sprawling home he wanted Ashley to see, they only had an hour of daylight left.

He pulled to the curb just before the bend in the private lane and shut the engine off. Beside him Ashley's brow furrowed in obvious confusion.

He walked around to her side of the car and opened the door. He pulled her out, carefully arranged her scarf and cap so she'd be warm and then took her hand and tugged her onto the road.

Snow drifted in the ditches and spread out over the landscape, a pristine covering of sheer white. It reminded him of her. Magical, almost like a fairy tale.

He'd once told her that life wasn't a fairy tale, but damn it, she was going to have one. Starting right now.

"It's beautiful here," she said breathlessly.

Enchantment filled her eyes as she stared out over the rolling hills. Her face had softened into a dreamy smile and he felt a stirring in his heart. This was how he wanted her to look every day. Happy. Sparkling. So damn beautiful she made him ache to his bones.

He pulled her up short just as they reached the sharp bend in the road. He kept hold of her hand and pulled her to face him, his heart pounding damn near out of his chest.

Their breaths came out in visible puffs. Snowflakes began to fall again, spiraling lazily down, some sticking in her hair, some melting and absorbed by the splash of sun in the barren white of winter.

"Ash."

It came out as a croak and he cleared his throat, prepared to fight with everything he had to keep the woman he loved.

She cocked her head to the side and sent him an inquisitive glance.

"Yes, Devon?"

Her voice was sweet and clear in the silence that had settled over the area. Only the distant crack of a tree limb disturbed the calm.

He hated that he stood here, tongue-tied, unable to form a single damn word, his heart in knots. There was so much to say he simply didn't know where to start. Finally his frustration got the better of him.

"Damn it, I love you. I'm standing here trying my best to come up with the words to everything I have to say and all I can think, all that weighs on my mind, is that I love you so damn much and I can't live without you. Don't make me live without you, Ash."

Her expressive eyes widened in shock. Her mouth popped open and then snapped shut again. She shook her head wordlessly as if she had no idea what to say to his sudden declaration.

Then hurt entered her eyes, crushing him with the weight of her pain. Her gaze held the memory of all the terrible things he'd said and done. He couldn't breathe for wanting to drop to his knees and beg her forgiveness.

"Then why?" she choked out. "If you love me, really love *me*, then why would you want me to change? You don't love the real me, Dev. You love the image you have in your head of how the perfect wife should be. Well, I've got news for you. I'm not her. I'll never be her."

She was glorious in her anger. Her eyes came to life and sparked darts of fire. Color suffused her cheeks and her lips pinched together as she glared holes through him.

"Trying to change you was the biggest mistake I've ever

made or will make in my life. God, Ash, when I think of how stupid I was I just want to punch something."

He put his hands on her shoulders and stared intently into her eyes. "You are the most beautiful, precious thing that has ever barreled into my life. I didn't see it because I didn't want to see it. When your father suggested the marriage, I was pissed and I resented his interference."

"That makes two of us," Ashley muttered.

"But the thing was, I didn't mind the idea of marrying you. Even when I told myself that I was angry, there was a part of me that didn't at all mind the idea of marriage and settling down. Starting a family. With you.

"I was torn and I was an immature jerk acting out because I felt like marriage was being forced on me instead of when I was ready for it. Even though I didn't mind the outcome, I was resentful on principle. Which is stupid. And then on our honeymoon night I was gutted when you found out because the last thing I ever wanted was to hurt you. I felt cornered. Here you were demanding to know how I felt and my feelings weren't even something I could admit to myself. So I answered out of frustration and I said all that crap about how we could have a good marriage anyway because in my mind I wanted things to go on as they had before but without the vulnerability I felt every time the question of love popped up."

He sighed and released her shoulders, stepping back for a moment as he stared off into the distance. "Your entire family baffles me, Ash. I don't always know how to take them. I'm not used to having this big, huge loving family where dysfunction isn't a way of life. Your dad was always calling me 'son,' and he wanted me to marry you, and all I could think was that I don't fit here. I'm not good enough. I wasn't worthy. And that made me angry because after I left home, I was determined never to feel inferior again."

She was still staring at him like she had no idea what to say.

"You scared me, Ash. You barged into my life, turned it

upside down with your take-no-prisoners attitude. You were the one thing I couldn't control, couldn't put in its proper place, and I tried. Oh, I tried. I was determined that you weren't going to be a threat to me. I hated how rattled you made me feel and how I went soft every time you entered a room. I thought somehow if I covered you up that you wouldn't shine quite so brightly and that maybe I could better control my reaction to you or at least I wouldn't feel like my guts had been ripped out every time you smiled at me."

"Wow," she whispered. "I have no idea what to say, Devon. I had no idea I affected you so badly."

He shook his head. "Oh, God, no, Ash. Don't you see? You are the very best part of me. It wasn't you. It was never you. It was me."

No longer able to keep his hands from her, he stepped forward again and pulled her close so that their faces were almost touching and he could feel the warmth of her breath on his throat.

"You are the very best part of my world. You are my life. I cannot imagine an existence without you. I don't want to. What I did was unforgivable. It was the result of ignorance and stupidity of the highest magnitude. I can only tell you that if you let me back into your life that you'll never have cause to doubt me again. I'll spend every single day proving to you that you are the absolute center of my universe. You wanted a man who adored you beyond reason. Someone who accepted you for the beautiful, amazing woman that you are. Look no further, Ash. He's standing in front of you with his heart in his hands. No man will ever love you more than I do. It isn't possible."

Her eyes were huge in her face. Brilliantly blue, sparkling like the most exquisite gems. Her cheeks were brushed with rose and her throat worked up and down as she swallowed. Tears glittered like diamonds, clung to her lashes but didn't fall. He wouldn't let them this time. If she never cried again, it would be too soon for him.

When she opened her mouth to speak, he simply put his lips to hers and kissed her long and sweet. He was shaking as he crushed her to him. For the last week he'd despaired of ever getting this close to her again and now she was warm and soft in his arms and so very precious.

"Don't say anything yet," he whispered. "There's still something I want to show you."

He pulled away, gathered her hand in his and pulled her along the road. She walked with him haltingly, as if she were in a solid daze. As they rounded the sharp bend, she stopped in her tracks and gazed in wonder at the sprawling house on top of the hill.

In the distance, dogs barked and she turned her head, her brow furrowing as she searched for the source of the noise. And then over the hill, two dogs bounded, making a beeline for Ashley.

"Mac! Paulina!"

She dropped to her knees just as the dogs launched themselves at her, licking and barking excitedly as Ashley tried to hug them.

"Oh my God, where did you come from?" she whispered.

Devon glanced up the hill to see Cam standing there and Devon waved his thanks before turning his attention back to Ashley and the sheer joy in her eyes.

One of the dogs knocked her over and she went laughing to the ground, snow sticking to her coat as she lay gasping for air.

Devon carefully picked her back up and fended off the animals as they tried their best to lick her to death.

"They come with the house," he said solemnly. "Since you're the new director of the shelter, it only stood to reason that some of the animals find their home here."

She brushed herself off and then stared back at the house again. "Is it... Is it yours?" she asked hesitantly.

"No, it's yours."

She turned to stare at him, excitement flashing like fireworks in her eyes. "You mean it? Really? How? Why? When?"

He chuckled indulgently and then because he couldn't help himself, he pulled her into his arms so that he was wrapped solidly around her. They stood staring up at the house as her heart beat solidly against his chest.

"You wanted a home where you could envision children playing and you could be surrounded by your animals. I ignored that because I wasn't ready for anything in my life to change. My apartment was comfortable and I saw no reason we couldn't live there. But the simple truth is, I want to live wherever you are and wherever makes you happy. A good friend told me to go big or go home. I'm going big, Ash. Because I'll do any damn thing in the world to have you back in my life."

"Oh my," she whispered. "I don't know what to say, Dev. You're saying everything I've ever dreamed you saying. I want to believe you. I want it more than anything. But I'm afraid."

He tugged her even closer and rested his forehead on hers. "I love you, Ash. That isn't going to change. I was an ass. I just need a chance to prove to you that you're safe with me and a chance to show you that I'll love and cherish you every day for the rest of your life. You and our children."

"You're okay with the baby?"

"If I was any more okay, I'd burst wide open. I can't think of anything better than this house with you and our son or daughter plus the half dozen or so more we'll fill it with."

"Oh I love that," she said, her eyes lighting up like a thousand suns.

He stroked a strand of her hair away from her face and then he kissed her softly, lingering over her lips as he savored being this close to her again.

"I love you," he said. "I love you more than I ever thought it possible to love another person. I won't lie. It scares the hell out of me, but being without you scares me even more. Give us a chance, Ash. I'll show you that you can trust me again. I swear it."

She wrapped her arms around his shoulders and moved her

forehead down to nestle in the side of his neck. "I love you too, Dev. So very much. You have the power to hurt me like no one else. But you also have the power to make me happier than anyone else in the world."

He inhaled the scent of her hair and hugged her more fiercely. "I want you to be happy. I want you to smile again. I'll do anything to make that happen."

She pulled away and smiled mischievously up at him as the dogs danced around at their heels. "Then why don't you show me my new house?"

He relaxed, going suddenly weak as relief tore through him with the force of a storm. Oh, God. He couldn't even find his tongue because he feared if he tried to speak right now, he'd lose what was left of his composure.

It was several long seconds before he could pull himself together enough to speak.

"The sale isn't final yet but the house has been empty for six months and I've gotten the keys. I'll be happy to show you around."

She threaded her arm through his as they started up the rest of the driveway leading to the house.

"Can't you just imagine our children playing here?" she said wistfully. "And the dogs running after them?"

He pulled his arm loose and wrapped it tightly around her as he leaned down to kiss her temple.

"Know what the best part will be?"

She glanced up at him in question.

"Seeing their mother's smile light up their father's world each and every day of his life."

* * * * *

Turn the page for an exclusive short story
by Brenda Jackson
NEVER TOO LATE

NEVER TOO LATE
Brenda Jackson

One

Twelve days and counting...

Pushing a lock of twisted hair behind her ear, Sienna Bradford, soon to become Sienna Davis once again, straightened her shoulders as she walked into the cabin she'd once shared with her husband—soon-to-be ex-husband.

She glanced around. Had it been just three years ago when Dane had brought her here for the first time? Three years ago when the two of them had sat there in front of the fireplace after making love, and planned their wedding? Promising that no matter what, their marriage would last forever? She took a deep breath knowing for them, forever would end in twelve days in Judge Ratcliff's chambers.

Just thinking about it made her heart ache, but she decided it wouldn't help matters to have a pity-party. What was done was done and things just hadn't worked out between her and Dane liked they'd hoped. There was nothing to do now but move on with her life. But first, according to a letter her attorney had received from Dane's attorney a few days ago, she had ten days to clear out any and all of her belongings from the cabin, and the sooner she got the task done the better. Dane had agreed to let her keep the condo if she returned full ownership of the cabin to him. She'd had no problem with that since he had owned it before they married.

Sienna crossed the room, shaking off the March chill. According to forecasters, a snowstorm was headed toward the Smoky Mountains within the next seventy-two hours, which meant she had to hurry and pack up her stuff and take the two-hour drive back to Charlotte. Once she got home she intended to stay inside and curl up in bed with a good book. Sienna smiled, thinking that a "do nothing" weekend was just what she needed in her too-frantic life.

Her smile faded when she considered that since starting her own interior decorating business a year and a half ago, she'd been extremely busy—and she had to admit that was when her marital problems with Dane had begun.

Sienna took a couple of steps toward the bedroom to begin packing her belongings when she heard the sound of the door opening. Turning quickly, she suddenly remembered she had forgotten to lock the door. Not smart when she was alone in a secluded cabin high up in the mountains, and a long way from civilization.

A scream quickly died in her throat when the person who walked in—standing a little over six feet with dark eyes, close-cropped black hair, chestnut coloring and a medium build—was none other than her soon-to-be-ex.

From the glare on his face, she could tell he wasn't happy to see her. But so what? She wasn't happy to see him, either, and couldn't help wondering why he was here.

Before she could swallow the lump in her throat to ask, he crossed his arms over his broad chest, intensified his glare and said in that too-sexy voice she knew so well, "I thought that was your car parked outside, Sienna. What are you doing here?"

Two

Dane wet his suddenly dry lips and immediately decided he needed a beer. Lucky for him there was a six-pack in the refrigerator from the last time he'd come to the cabin. But he didn't intend on moving an inch until Sienna told him what she was doing here.

She was nervous, he could tell. Well, that was too friggin' bad. She was the one who'd filed for the divorce, he hadn't. But since she had made it clear that she wanted him out of her life, he had no problem giving her what she wanted even if the pain was practically killing him. But she'd never know that.

"What do you think I'm doing here?" she asked smartly, reclaiming his absolute attention.

"If I knew, I wouldn't have asked," he said, giving her the same unblinking stare. And to think that at one time he actually thought she was his whole world. At some point during their marriage she had changed and transitioned into quite a character—someone he was certain he didn't know anymore.

She met his gaze for a long, level moment before placing her hands on her hips. Doing so drew his attention to her body, a body he'd seen naked countless times, a body he knew as well as his own, a body he used to ease into during the heat of passion to receive pleasure so keen and satisfying, just thinking about it made him hard.

"The reason I'm here, Dane Bradford, is because your attorney sent mine this nasty little letter demanding that I remove my stuff within ten days, and this weekend was better than next weekend. However, no thanks to you, I still had to close the shop early to beat traffic and the bad weather."

He actually smiled at the thought of her having to do that. "And I bet it almost killed you to close your shop early. Heaven forbid. You probably had to cancel a couple of appointments. Something I could never get you to do for me."

Sienna rolled her eyes. They'd had this same argument over and over again and it all boiled down to the same thing. He thought her job meant more to her than he did because of all the time she'd put into it. But what really irked her with that accusation was that before she'd even entertained the idea of quitting her job and embarking on her own business, they had talked about it and what it would mean. She would have to work her butt off and network to build a new clientele, and then there would be time spent working on decorating proposals, spending long hours in many beautiful homes of the rich and famous. And he had understood and had been supportive…at least in the beginning.

But then he began complaining that she was spending too much time away from home, away from him. Things only got worse from there, and now she was a woman who had gotten married at twenty-four and was getting divorced at twenty-seven.

"Look, Dane, it's too late to look back, reflect and complain. In twelve days you'll be free of me and I'll be free of you. I'm sure there's a woman out there who has the time and patience to—"

"Now that's a word you don't know the meaning of, Sienna," Dane interrupted. "Patience. You were always in a rush, and your tolerance level for the least little thing was zero. Yeah, I know I probably annoyed the hell out of you at times. But then there were times you annoyed me, as well. Neither of us is perfect."

Sienna let out a deep breath. "I never said I was perfect, Dane."

"No, but you sure as hell acted like you thought you were, didn't you?"

Three

Dane's question struck a nerve. Considering her background, how could he assume Sienna thought she was perfect? She had come from a dysfunctional family if ever there was one. Her mother hadn't loved her father. Her father loved all women except her mother. And neither seemed to love their only child. Sienna had always combated lack of love by doing the right thing, thinking that if she did, her parents would eventually love her. It didn't work. But still, she had gone through high school and college being the good girl, thinking being good would eventually pay off and earn her the love she'd always craved.

In her mind, it had when she'd met Dane, the man least likely to fall in love with her. He was the son of the millionaire Bradfords who'd made money in land development. She hadn't been his family's choice and they made sure she knew it every chance they got. Whenever she was around them they made her feel inadequate, like she didn't measure up to their society friends, and since she didn't come from a family with a prestigious background, she wasn't good enough for their son.

She bet they wished they'd never hired the company she'd been working for to decorate their home. That's how she and Dane had met. She'd been going over fabric swatches with his mother and he'd walked in after playing a game of tennis. The rest was history. But the question of the hour was, had she been so busy trying to succeed the past year and a half, trying to be the perfect business owner, that she had eventually alienated the one person who'd mattered most to her?

"Can't answer that, can you?" Dane said, breaking into her thoughts. "Maybe that will give you something to think about twelve days from now when you put your John Hancock on the divorce papers. Now if you'll excuse me, I have something to do," he said, walking around her toward the bedroom.

"Wait. You never said why *you're* here?"

He stopped. The intensity of his gaze sent shivers of heat through her entire body. And it didn't help matters that he was wearing jeans and a dark brown leather bomber jacket that made him look sexy as hell...as usual. "I was here a couple of weekends ago and left something behind. I came to get it."

"Were you alone?" The words had rushed out before she could hold them back and immediately she wanted to smack herself. The last thing she wanted was for him to think she cared...even if she did.

He hooked his thumbs in his jeans and continued to hold her gaze. "Would it matter to you if I weren't?"

She couldn't look at him, certain he would see her lie when she replied, "No, it wouldn't matter. What you do is none of my business."

"That's what I thought." And then he walked off toward the bedroom and closed the door.

Sienna frowned. That was another thing she didn't like about Dane. He never stayed around to finish one of their arguments. Thanks to her parents she was a pro at it, but Dane would always walk away after giving some smart parting remark that only made her that much angrier. He didn't know how to fight fair. He didn't know how to fight at all. He'd come from a family too dignified for such nonsense.

Moving toward the kitchen to see if there was anything of hers in there, Sienna happened to glance out of the window.

"Oh my God," she said, rushing over to the window. It was snowing already. No, it wasn't just snowing, there was a full-scale blizzard going on outside. What happened to the seventy-two hour warning?

She heard Dane when he came out of the bedroom. He looked beyond her and out the window, uttering one hell of a curse word before quickly walking to the door, slinging it open and stepping outside.

In just that short period of time, everything was beginning to turn white. The last time they'd had a sudden snowstorm such as this had been a few years ago. It had been so bad the media had nicknamed it the "Beast from the East."

It seemed the beast was back, and it had turned downright spiteful. Not only was it acting ugly outside, it had placed Sienna in one hell of a predicament. She was stranded in a cabin in the Smoky Mountains with her soon-to-be-ex. Things couldn't get any more bizarre than that.

Four

Moments later when Dane stepped back into the cabin, slamming the door behind him, Sienna could tell he was so mad he could barely breathe.

"What's wrong, Dane? You're being forced to cancel a date tonight?" she asked snidely. A part of her was still upset at the thought that he might have brought someone here a couple of weekends ago when they weren't officially divorced yet. The mere fact they had been separated for six months didn't count. She hadn't gone out with anyone. Indulging in a relationship with another man hadn't even crossed her mind.

He took a step toward her and she refused to back up. She was determined to maintain her ground and her composure, although the intense look in his eyes was causing crazy things to happen to her body, like it normally did whenever they were alone for any period of time. There may have been a number of things wrong with their marriage, but lack of sexual chemistry had never been one of them.

"Do you know what this means?" he asked, his voice shaking in anger.

She tilted her head to one side. "Other than I'm being forced to remain here with you for a couple of hours, no, I don't know what it means."

She saw his hands ball into fists at his side and knew he was probably fighting the urge to strangle her. "We're not talking about hours, Sienna. Try days. Haven't you been listening to the weather reports?"

She glared at him. "Haven't you? I'm not here by myself."

"Yes, but I thought I could come up here and in ten minutes max get what I came for and leave before the bad weather kicked in."

Sienna regretted that she hadn't been listening to the weather reports, at least not in detail. She'd known that a snowstorm was headed toward the mountains within seventy-two hours, which was why she'd thought like Dane that she had time to rush and get in and out before the nasty weather hit. Anything other than that, she was clueless. And what was he saying about them being up here for days instead of hours? "Yes, I did listen to the weather reports, but evidently I missed something."

He shook his head. "Evidently you missed a lot if you think this storm is going to blow over in a couple of hours. According to forecasters, what you see isn't the worst of it, and because of that unusual cold front hovering about in the east, it may last for days."

She swallowed deeply. The thought of spending *days* alone in a cabin with Dane didn't sit well with her. "How many days are we talking about?"

"Try three or four."

She didn't want to try any at all, and as she continued to gaze into his eyes she saw a look of worry replace the anger in their dark depths. Then she knew what had him upset.

"Do we have enough food and supplies up here to hold us for three or four days?" she asked, as she began to nervously gnaw on her lower lip. The magnitude of the situation they were in was slowly dawning on her, and when he didn't answer immediately she knew they were in trouble.

Five

Dane saw the panic that suddenly lined Sienna's face. He wished he could say he didn't give a damn, but there was no way that he could. This woman would always matter to him whether she was married to him or not. From the moment he had walked into his father's study that day and their gazes had connected, he had known then, as miraculous at it had seemed, and without a word spoken between them, that he was meant to love her. And for a while he had convinced her of that, but not anymore. Evidently, at some point during their marriage she began believing otherwise.

"Dane?"

He rubbed his hand down his face, trying to get his thoughts together. Given the situation they were in, he knew honesty was foremost. But then he'd always been honest with her; however, he doubted she could say the same for herself. "To answer your question, Sienna, I'm not sure. Usually I keep the place well stocked with everything, but like I said earlier, I was here a couple of weekends ago, and I used a lot of the supplies then."

He refused to tell her that, in a way, it had been her fault. Receiving those divorce papers had driven him here, to wallow in self-pity, vent out his anger and drink his pain away with a bottle of Johnny Walker Red. "I guess we need to go check things out," he said, trying not to get as worried as she was beginning to look.

He followed her into the kitchen, trying not to watch the sway of her hips as she walked in front of him. The hot, familiar sight of her in a pair of jeans and a pullover sweater had him cursing under his breath and summoning up a quick remedy for the situation he found himself in. The thought of being stranded for any amount of time with Sienna wasn't good.

He stopped walking when she flung open the refrigerator. His six-pack of beer was still there, but little else. But then he wasn't studying the contents of the refrigerator as much as he was studying her. She was bent over, looking inside, but all he could think of was another time he had walked into this kitchen and found her in that same position, and wearing nothing more than his T-shirt that had barely covered her bottom. It hadn't taken much for him to go into a crazed fit of lust and quickly remove his pajama bottoms and take her right then and there, against the refrigerator, giving them both the orgasm of a lifetime.

"Thank goodness there are some eggs in here," she said, intruding on his heated trip down memory lane. "About half a dozen. And there's a loaf of bread that looks edible. There's some kind of meat in the freezer, but I'm not sure what it is, though. Looks like chicken."

She turned around and her pouty mouth tempted him to kiss it, devour it and make her moan. He watched her sigh deeply and then she gave him a not-so-hopeful gaze and said, "Our rations don't look good, Dane. What are we going to do?"

Six

Sienna's breath caught when the corners of Dane's mouth tilted in an irresistible smile. She'd seen the look before. She knew that smile, and she also recognized that bulge pressing against his zipper. She frowned. "Don't even think it, Dane."

He leaned back against the kitchen counter. Hell, he wanted to do more than think it, he wanted to do it. But, of course, he would pretend he hadn't a clue as to what she was talking about. "What?"

Her frown deepened. "And don't act all innocent with me. I know what you were thinking."

A smile tugged deeper at Dane's lips, knowing she probably did. There were some things a man couldn't hide and a rock solid hard-on was one of them. He decided not to waste his time and hers pretending the chemistry between them was dead when they both knew it was still very much alive. "Don't ask me to apologize. It's not my fault you have so much sex appeal and my desire for you is automatic, even when we're headed for divorce court."

Dane saying the word *divorce* was a stark reminder that their life together, as they once knew it, would be over in twelve days. "Let's get back to important matters, Dane, like our survival. On a positive note, we might be able to make do if we cut back on meals, which may be hard for you with your ferocious appetite."

A wicked-sounding chuckle poured from his throat. "Which one?"

Sienna swallowed as her pulse pounded in response to Dane's question. She was quickly reminded, although she wished there was some way she could forget, that her husband...or soon-to-be-ex...did have two appetites. One was of a gastric nature and the other purely sexual. Thoughts of the purely sexual one had intense heat radiating all through her. Dane had devoured every inch of her body in ways she didn't even want to think about. Especially not now.

She placed her hands on her hips knowing he was baiting her, really doing a hell of a lot more than that. He was stirring up feelings inside of her that were making it hard for her to think straight. "Get serious, Dane."

"I am." He then came to stand in front of her. "Did you bring anything with you?"

She lifted a brow. "Anything like what?"

"Stuff to snack on. You're good for that. How you do it without gaining a pound is beyond me."

She shrugged, refusing to tell him that she used to work it off with all those in-bed, out-of-bed exercises they used to do. If he hadn't noticed then she wouldn't tell him that in six months without him in her bed she had gained five pounds. "I might have a candy bar or two in the car."

He smiled. "That's all?"

She rolled her eyes upward. "Okay, okay, I might have a couple of bags of chips, too." She decided not to mention the three boxes of Girl Scout cookies that had been purchased that morning from a little girl standing in front of a grocery store.

"I hadn't planned to spend the night here, Dane. I had merely thought I could quickly pack things and leave."

He nodded. "Okay, I'll get the snacks from your car while I'm outside checking on some wood we'll need for the fire. The power is still on, but I can't see that lasting too much longer. I wish I would have gotten that generator fixed."

Her eyes widened in alarm. "You didn't?"

"No. So you might want to go around and gather up all the candles you can. And there should be a box of matches in one of these drawers."

"Okay."

Dane turned to leave. He then turned back around. She was nibbling on her bottom lip as he assumed she would be. "And stop worrying. We're going to make it."

When he walked out of the room, Sienna leaned back against the closed refrigerator thinking those were the exact words he'd said to her three years ago when he had asked her to marry him. Now she *was* worried because they didn't have a proven track record.

Seven

After putting on the snow boots he kept at the cabin, Dane made his way outdoors, grateful for the time he wouldn't be in Sienna's presence. Being around her and still loving her like he did was hard. Even now, he didn't know the reason for the divorce, other than what was noted in the papers he'd been served that day a few weeks ago. Irreconcilable differences—whatever the hell that was supposed to mean.

Sienna hadn't come to him so they could talk about any problems they were having. He had come home one day and she had moved out. He still was at a loss as to what could have been so wrong with their marriage that she could no longer see a future for them.

He would always recall that time as being the lowest point in his life. For days it was as if a part of him was missing. It had taken a while to finally pull himself together and realize she wasn't coming back no matter how many times he'd asked her to. And all it took was the receipt of that divorce petition to make him realize that Sienna wanted him out of her life, and actually believed that whatever issues were keeping them apart couldn't be resolved.

A little while later Dane had gathered more wood to put with the huge stack already on the back porch, glad that if nothing else they wouldn't freeze to death. The cabin was equipped with enough toiletries to hold them for at least a week, which was a good thing. And he hadn't wanted to break the news to Sienna that the meat in the freezer wasn't chicken, but deer meat that one of his clients had given him a couple of weeks ago after a hunting trip. It was good to eat, but he knew Sienna well enough to know she would have to be starving before she would consume any of it.

After rubbing his icy hands on his jeans, he stuck them into his pockets to keep them from freezing. Walking around the house, he strolled over to her car, opened the door and found the candy bars, chips and…Girl Scout cookies, he noted, lifting a brow. She hadn't mentioned them, and he saw they were her favorite kind, as well as his. He quickly recalled the first year they were married and how they shared the cookies as a midnight snack after making love. He couldn't help but smile as he remembered that night and others where they had spent time together, not just in bed but cooking in the kitchen, going to movies, concerts, parties, having picnics and just plain sitting around and talking for hours.

He suddenly realized that one of the things that had been missing from their marriage for a while was communication. When had they stopped talking? The first thought that grudgingly came to mind was when she'd begun bringing work home, letting it intrude on what had always been their time together. That's when they had begun living in separate worlds.

Dane breathed in deeply. He wanted to get back into Sienna's world and he definitely wanted her back in his. He didn't want a divorce. He wanted to keep his wife, but he refused to resort to any type of manipulating, dominating or controlling tactics to do it. What he and Sienna needed was to use this weekend to keep it honest and talk openly about what had gone wrong with their marriage. They would go further by finding ways to resolve things. He still loved her and wanted to believe that deep down she still loved him.

There was only one way to find out.

Eight

Sienna glanced around the room seeing all the lit candles and thinking just how romantic they made the cabin look. Taking a deep breath, she frowned in irritation, thinking that romance should be the last thing on her mind. Dane was her soon-to-be ex-husband. Whatever they once shared was over, done with, had come to a screeching end.

If only the memories weren't so strong...

She glanced out the window and saw him piling wood on the back porch. Never in her wildest dreams would she have thought her day would end up this way, with her and Dane being stranded together at the cabin—a place they always considered as their favorite getaway spot. During the first two years of their marriage, they would come here every chance they got, but in the past year she could recall them coming only once. Somewhere along the way she had stopped allowing them time even for this.

She sighed deeply recalling how important it had been to her at the beginning of their marriage for them to make time to talk about matters of interest, whether trivial or important. They had always been attuned to each other and Dane had always been a good listener, which to her conveyed a sign of caring and respect. But the last couple of times they had tried to talk ended up with them snapping at each other, which only built bitterness and resentment.

The lights blinked and she knew they were about to go out. She was glad that she had taken the initiative to go into the kitchen and scramble up some eggs earlier. And she was inwardly grateful that if she had to get stranded in the cabin during a snowstorm that Dane was here with her. Heaven knows she would have been a basket case had she found herself up here alone.

The lights blinked again before finally going out, but the candles provided the cabin with plenty of light. Not sure if the temperatures outside would cause the pipes to freeze, she had run plenty of water in the bathtub and kitchen sink, and filled every empty jug with water for them to drink. She'd also found batteries to put in the radio so they could keep up with any reports on the weather.

"I saw the lights go out. Are you okay?"

Sienna turned around. Dane was leaning in the doorway with his hands stuck in the pockets of his jeans. The pose made him look incredibly sexy. "Yes, I'm okay. I was able to get the candles all lit and there are plenty more."

"That's good."

"Just in case the pipes freeze and we can't use the shower, I filled the bathtub with water so we can take a bath that way." At his raised brow she quickly added, "Separately, of course. And I made sure I filled plenty of bottles of drinking water, too."

He nodded. "Sounds like you've been busy."

"So have you. I saw through the window when you put all that wood on the porch. It will probably come in handy."

He moved away from the door. "Yes, and with the electricity out I need to go ahead and get the fire started."

Sienna swallowed as she watched him walk toward her on his way to the fireplace, and not for the first time she thought about how remarkably handsome he was. He had that certain charisma that made women get hot all over just looking at him.

It suddenly occurred to her that he'd already got a fire started, and the way it was spreading through her was about to make her burst into flames.

Nine

"You okay?" Dane asked Sienna as he walked toward her with a smile.

She nodded and cleared her throat. "Yes, why do you ask?"

"Because you're looking at me funny."

"Oh." She was vaguely aware of him walking past her to kneel in front of the fireplace. She turned and watched him, saw him move the wood around before taking a match and lighting it to start a fire. He was so good at kindling things, whether wood or the human body.

"If you like, I can make something for dinner," she decided to say; otherwise she would continue to stand there and say nothing while staring at him. It was hard trying to be normal in a rather awkward situation.

"What are our options?" he asked without looking around.

She chuckled. "An egg sandwich and tea. I made both earlier before the power went off."

He turned at that and his gaze caught hers. A smile crinkled his eyes. "Do I have a choice?"

"Not if you want to eat."

"What about those Girl Scout cookies I found in your car?"

Her eyes narrowed. "They're off-limits. You can have one of the candy bars, but the cookies are mine."

His mouth broke into a wide grin. "You have enough cookies to share so stop being selfish."

He turned back around and she made a face at him behind his back. He was back to stoking the fire and her gaze went to his hands. Those hands used to be the giver of so much pleasure and almost ran neck and neck with his mouth…but not quite. His mouth was in a class by itself. But still, she could recall those same hands, gentle, provoking, moving all over her body, touching her everywhere and doing things to her that mere hands weren't suppose to do. However, she never had any complaints.

"Did you have any plans for tonight, Sienna?"

His words intruded into her heated thoughts. "No, why?"

"Just wondering. You thought I had a date tonight. What about you?"

She shrugged. "No. As far as I'm concerned, until we sign those final papers I'm still legally married and wouldn't feel right going out with someone."

He turned around and locked his eyes with hers. "I know what you mean," he said. "I wouldn't feel right going out with someone else."

Heat seeped through her every pore with his words. "So you haven't been dating, either?"

"No."

There were a number of questions she wanted to ask him—how he spent his days, his nights, what his family thought of their pending divorce, what he thought of it, was he ready for it to be over for them to go their separate ways—but there was no way she could ask him any of those things. "I guess I'll go put dinner on the table."

He chuckled. "An egg sandwich and tea?"

"Yes." She turned to leave.

"Sienna?"

She turned back around. "Yes?"

"I don't like being stranded, but since I am, I'm glad it's with you."

For a moment she couldn't say anything, then she cleared her throat while backing up a couple of steps. "Ah, yeah right, same here." She backed up some more then said, "I'll go set out the food now." And then she turned and quickly left the room.

Ten

Sienna glanced up and smiled when she heard Dane walk into the kitchen. "Your feast awaits you."

"Whoopee."

She laughed. "Hey, I know the feeling. I'm glad I had a nice lunch today in celebration. I took on a new client."

Dane came and joined her at the table. "Congratulations."

"Thank you."

She took a bite of her scrambled egg sandwich and a sip of her tea and then said, "It's been a long time since you seemed genuinely pleased with my accomplishments."

He glanced up after taking a sip of his own tea and stared at her for a moment. "I know and I'm sorry about that. It was hard being replaced by your work, Sienna."

She lifted her head and stared at him, met his gaze. She saw the tightness of his jaw and the firm set of his mouth. He actually believed that something could replace him with her, and knowing that hit a raw and sensitive nerve. "My work never replaced you, Dane. Why did you begin feeling that way?"

Dane leaned back in his chair, tilted his head slightly. He was more than mildly surprised with her question. It was then he realized that she really didn't know. Hadn't a clue. This was the opportunity that he wanted, what he was hoping they would have. Now was the time to put aside anger, bitterness, foolish pride and whatever else was working at destroying their marriage. Now was the time for complete honesty. "You started missing dinner. Not once but twice, sometimes three times a week. Eventually, you stopped making excuses and didn't show up."

What he'd said was the truth. "But I was working and taking on new clients," she defended. "You said you would understand."

"And I did for a while and up to a point. But there is such a thing as common courtesy and mutual respect, Sienna. In the end, I felt like I'd been thrown by the wayside, that you didn't care anymore about us, our love or our marriage."

She narrowed her eyes. "And why didn't you say something?"

"When? I was usually asleep when you got home and when I got up in the morning you were too sleepy to discuss anything. I invited you to lunch several times, but you couldn't fit me into your schedule."

"I had appointments."

"Yes, and I always felt because of it that your clients were more important."

"Still, I wished you would have let me know how you felt," she said, after taking another sip of tea.

"I did, several times. But you weren't listening."

She sighed deeply. "We used to know how to communicate."

"Yes, at one time we did, didn't we?" Dane said quietly. "But I'm also to blame for the failure of our marriage, our lack of communication. And then there were the problems you were having with my parents. When it came to you, I never hesitated letting my parents know when they were out of line and that I wouldn't put up with their treatment of you. But then I felt that at some point you needed to start believing that what they thought didn't matter and stand up to them.

"I honestly thought I was doing the right thing when I decided to just stay out of it and give you the chance to deal with them, to finally put them in their place. Instead, you let them erode your security and confidence to the point where you felt you had to prove you were worthy of them…and of me. That's what drove you to be so successful, wasn't it, Sienna? Feeling the need to prove something is what working all those long hours is all about, isn't it?"

Eleven

Sienna quickly got up from the table and walked to the window. It was turning dark but she could clearly see that things hadn't let up. It was still snowing outside, worse than an hour before. She tried to concentrate on what was beyond that window and not on the question Dane had asked her.

"Sienna?"

Moments later she turned back around to face Dane, knowing he was waiting on her response. "What do you want me to say, Dane? Trust me, you don't want to get me started since you've always known how your family felt about me."

His brow furrowed sharply as he moved from the table to join her at the window, coming to stand directly in front of her. "And you've known it didn't matter one damn iota. Why would you let it continue to matter to you?"

She shook her head, tempted to bare her soul but fighting not to. "But you don't understand how important it was for your family to accept me, to love me."

Dane stepped closer, looked into eyes that were fighting to keep tears at bay. "Wasn't my love enough, Sienna? I'd told you countless times that you didn't marry my family, you married me. I'm not proud of the fact that my parents think too highly of themselves and our family name at times, but I've constantly told you it didn't matter. Why can't you believe me?"

When she didn't say anything, he sighed deeply. "You've been around people with money before. Do all of them act like my parents?"

She thought of her best friend's family. The Steeles. "No."

"Then what should that tell you? They're my parents. I know that they aren't close to being perfect, but I love them."

"And I never wanted to do anything to make you stop loving them."

He reached up and touched her chin. "And that's what this is about, isn't it? Why you filed for a divorce. You thought that you could."

Sienna angrily wiped at a tear she couldn't contain any longer. "I didn't ever want you to have to choose."

Dane's heart ached. Evidently she didn't know just how much he loved her. "There wouldn't have been a choice to make. You're my wife. I love you. I will always love you. When we married, we became one."

He leaned down and brushed a kiss on her cheek, then several. He wanted to devour her mouth, deepen the kiss and escalate it to the level he needed it to be, but he couldn't. He wouldn't. What they needed was to talk, to communicate, to try and fix whatever was wrong with their marriage. He pulled back. It was hard when he heard her soft sigh, her heated moan.

He gave in briefly to temptation and tipped her chin up and placed a kiss on her lips. "There's plenty of hot water still left in the tank," he said softly, stroking her chin. "Go ahead and take a shower before it gets completely dark, and then I'll take one."

He continued to stroke her chin when he added, "Then what I want is for us to do something we should have done months ago, Sienna. I want us to sit down and talk. And I mean to really talk, to regain that level of communication we once had. And what I need to know more than anything is whether my love will ever be enough for you."

Twelve

You're my wife. I love you. I will always love you. When we married, we became one.

Dane's words flowed through Sienna's mind as she stepped into the shower, causing a warm, fuzzy, glowing feeling to seep through her pores. Hope flared within her although she didn't want it to. She hadn't wanted to end her marriage, but when things had begun to get worse between her and Dane, she'd finally decided to take her in-laws' suggestion and get out of their son's life.

Even after three years of seeing how happy she and Dane were together, they still couldn't look beyond her past. They saw her as a nobody, a person who had married their son for his money. She had offered to sign a prenuptial agreement before the wedding and Dane had scoffed at the suggestion, refusing to even draw one up. But still, his parents had made it known each time they saw her just how much they resented the marriage.

And no matter how many times Dane had stood up to them

and had put them in their place regarding her, it would only be a matter of time before they resorted to their old ways again, though never in the presence of their son. Maybe Dane was right, and all she'd had to do was tell his parents off once and for all and that would have been the end of it. But she never could find the courage to do it.

And what was so hilarious with the entire situation was that she had basically become a workaholic to become successful in her own right so they could see her as their son's equal in every way, and in trying to impress them she had alienated Dane to the point that eventually he would have gotten fed up and asked her for a divorce if she hadn't done so first.

After spending time under the spray of water, she stepped out of the shower, intent on making sure there was enough hot water left for Dane. She tried to put out of her mind the last time she had taken a shower in this stall, and how Dane had joined her in it.

Toweling off, she was grateful she still had some of her belongings at the cabin to sleep in. The last thing she needed was to parade around Dane half naked. Then they would never get any talking done.

She slipped into a T-shirt and a pair of sweatpants she found in one of the drawers. Dane wanted to talk. How could they have honest communication without getting into a discussion about his parents again? She crossed her arms, trying to ignore the chill she was beginning to feel in the air. In order to stay warm they would both probably have to sleep in front of the fireplace tonight. She didn't want to think about what the possibility of doing something like that meant.

While her cell phone still had life, she decided to let her best friend, Vanessa Steele, know that she wouldn't be returning to Charlotte tonight. Dane was right. Not everyone with money acted like his parents. The Steeles, owners of a huge manufacturing company in Charlotte, were just as wealthy as the Bradfords. But they were as down-to-earth as people could get, which proved that not everyone with a lot of money were snobs.

"Hello?"

"Van, it's Sienna."

"Sienna, I was just thinking about you. Did you make it back before that snowstorm hit?"

"No, I'm stranded in the mountains."

"What! Do you want me to send my cousins to rescue you?"

Sienna smiled. Vanessa was talking about her four single male cousins, Chance, Sebastian, Morgan and Donovan Steele. Sienna had to admit that besides being handsome as sin, they were dependable to a fault. And of all people, she, Vanessa and Vanessa's two younger sisters, Taylor and Cheyenne, should know more than anyone since they had been notorious for getting into trouble while growing up, and the four brothers had always been there to bail them out.

"No, I don't need your cousins to come and rescue me."

"What about Dane? You know how I feel about you divorcing him, Sienna. He's still legally your husband and I think I should let him know where you are and let him decide if he should—"

"Vanessa," Sienna interrupted. "You don't have to let Dane know anything. He's here, stranded with me."

Thirteen

"How was your shower?" Dane asked Sienna when she returned to the living room a short while later.

"Great. Now it's your turn to indulge."

"Okay." Dane tried not to notice how the candlelight was flickering over Sienna's features, giving them an ethereal glow. He shoved his hands into the pockets of his jeans and for a long moment he stood there staring at her.

She lifted a brow. "What's wrong?"

"I was just thinking how incredibly beautiful you are."

Sienna breathed in deeply, trying to ignore the rush of sensations she felt from his words. "Thank you." Dane had always been a man who'd been free with his compliments. Being apart from him made her realize that was one of the things she missed, among many others.

"I'll be back in a little while," he said before leaving the room.

When he was gone, Sienna remembered the conversation she'd had with Vanessa earlier. Her best friend saw her and

Dane being stranded together on the mountain as a twist of fate that Sienna should use to her advantage. Vanessa further thought that for once, Sienna should stand up to the elder Bradfords and not struggle to prove herself to them. Dane had accepted her as she was and now it was time for her to be satisfied and happy with that. After all, she wasn't married to his parents.

A part of Sienna knew that Vanessa was right, but she had been seeking love from others for so long that she hadn't been able to accept that Dane's love was all the love she needed. Before her shower he had asked if his love was enough and now she knew that it was. It was past time for her to acknowledge that fact and to let him know it.

Dane stepped out of the shower and began toweling off. The bathroom carried Sienna's scent and the honeysuckle fragrance of the shower gel she enjoyed using.

Given their situation, he really should be worried about what they would be faced with if the weather didn't let up in a couple of days with the little bit of food they had. But for now, the thought of being stranded here with Sienna overrode all his concerns about that. In his heart he truly believed they would manage to get through any given situation. Now he had the task of convincing her of that.

He glanced down at his left hand and studied his wedding band. Two weeks ago when he had come here for his pity-party, he had taken it off in anger and thrown it in a drawer. It was only when he had returned to Charlotte that he realized he'd left it here in the cabin. At first he had shrugged it off as having no significant meaning since he would be a divorced man in a month's time anyway, but every day he'd felt that a part of him was missing.

In addition to reminding him of Sienna's absence from his life, to Dane, his ring signified their love and the vows that they had made, and a part of him refused to give that up. That's what had driven him back here this weekend—to reclaim the one element of his marriage that he refused to part with yet. Something he felt was rightfully his.

It seemed his ring wasn't the only thing he would get the chance to reclaim. More than anything, he wanted his wife back.

Fourteen

Dane walked into the living room and stopped in his tracks. Sienna sat in front of the fireplace, cross-legged, with a tray of cookies and two glasses of wine. He knew where the cookies had come from, but where the heck had she gotten the wine?

She must have heard him because she glanced over his way and smiled. At that moment he thought she was even more breathtaking than a rose in winter. She licked her lips and immediately he thought she was even more tempting than any decadent dessert.

He cleared his throat. "Where did the wine come from?"

She licked her lips again and his body responded in an unquestionable way. He hoped the candlelight was hiding the physical effect she was having on him. "I found it in one of the kitchen cabinets. I think it's the bottle that was left when we came here to celebrate our first anniversary."

He remembered that weekend. She had packed a selection of sexy lingerie and he had enjoyed removing each and every piece. She had also given him, among other things, a beautiful gold watch engraved with the inscription, *The Great Dane.* He, in turn, had given her a lover's bracelet, which was similar to a diamond tennis bracelet except that each letter of her name was etched in six of the stones.

He could still remember the single tear that had fallen from her eye when he had placed it on her wrist. That had been a special time for them, memories he would always cherish. That knowledge tightened the love that surrounded his heart. More than anything he was determined that they settle things this weekend. He needed to make her see that he was hers and she was his. For always.

His lips creased into a smile. "I see you've decided to share the cookies, after all," he said, crossing the room to her.

She chuckled as he dropped down on the floor beside her. "Either that or run the risk of you getting up during the night and eating them all." The firelight danced through the twists on her head, highlighting the medium brown coiled strands with golden flecks.

He absolutely loved the natural-looking hairstyle on her.

He lifted a dark brow. "Eating them all? Three boxes?"

Her smile grew soft. "Hey, you've been known to overindulge a few times."

He paused as heated memories consumed him, reminding him of those times he had overindulged, especially when it came to making love to her. He recalled one weekend they had gone at it almost nonstop. If she hadn't been on the pill there was no doubt in his mind that that single weekend would have made him a daddy. A very proud one at that.

She handed him a glass of wine. "May I propose a toast?"

His smile widened. "To what?"

"The return of the Beast from the East."

He switched his gaze from her to glance out the window. Even in the dark he could see the white flecks coming down in droves. He looked back at her and cocked a brow. "We have a reason to celebrate this bad weather?"

She stared at him for a long moment, then said quietly, "Yes. The beast is the reason we're stranded here together, and even with our low rations of food, I can't think of any other place I'd rather be...than here alone with you."

Fifteen

Dane stared at Sienna, and the intensity of that gaze made her entire body tingle, her nerve endings steam. It was pretty much like the day they'd met, when he'd walked into his father's study. She had looked up, their gazes had connected and the seriousness in the dark irises that had locked with hers had changed her life forever. She had fallen in love with him then and there.

Dane didn't say anything for a long moment as he continued to look at her, and then he lifted his wineglass and said huskily, "To the beast…who brought me Beauty."

His words were like a sensuous stroke down her spine, and the void feeling she'd had during the past few months was slowly fading away. After the toast was made and they had both taken sips of their wine, Dane placed his glass aside and then relieved her of hers. He then slowly leaned forward and captured her mouth, tasting the wine, relishing her delectable flavor. How had she gone without this for six months? How had she survived? She wondered as his tongue devoured hers, battering deep in the heat of her mouth, licking and sucking as he wove his tongue in and out between teeth, gums and whatever wanted to serve as a barrier.

He suddenly pulled back and stared at her. A smile touched the corners of his lips. "I could keep going and going, but before we go any further we need to talk, determine what brought us to this point so it won't ever be allowed to happen again. I don't want us to ever let anything or anyone have power over the vows we made three years ago."

Sienna nodded, thinking the way the firelight was dancing over his dark skin was sending an erotic frisson up her spine. "All right."

He stood. "I'll be right back."

Sienna lifted a brow, wondering where he was going, and watched as he crossed the room to open the desk drawer. Like her, he had changed into a T-shirt and a pair of sweats, and as she watched him she found it difficult to breathe. He moved in such a manly way, each movement a display of fine muscles and limbs and how they worked together in graceful coordination, perfect precision. Watching him knocked her hormones out of whack.

He returned moments later with pens and paper in hand. There was a serious expression on his face when he handed her a sheet of paper and a pen and kept the same for himself. "I want us to write down all the things we feel went wrong with our marriage, being honest and including everything. And then we'll discuss them."

She looked down at the pen and paper and then back at him. "You want me to write them down?"

"Yes, and I'll do the same."

Sienna nodded and watched as he began writing on his paper, wondering what he was jotting down. She leaned back and sighed, wondering if she could air their dirty laundry on paper, but it seemed he had no such qualms. Most couples sought the helpful guidance of marriage counselors when they found themselves in similar situations, but she hadn't given them that chance. But at this point, she would do anything to save her marriage.

So she began writing, being honest with herself and with him.

Sixteen

Dane finished writing and glanced over at Sienna. She was still at it and had a serious expression on her features. He studied the contours of her face. His gaze dropped to her neck, and he noticed the thin gold chain. She was still wearing the heart pendant he'd given her as a wedding gift.

Deep down, Dane believed this little assignment was what they needed as the first step in repairing what had gone wrong in their marriage. Having things written down would make it easier to stay focused and not go off on a tangent. And it made one less likely to give in to the power of the mind, the wills and the emotions. He wanted them to concentrate on those destructive elements and forces that had eroded away at what should have been a strong relationship.

She glanced up and met his gaze as she put the pen aside. She gave him a wry smile. "Okay, that's it."

He reached out and took her hand in his, tightening his hold on it when he saw a look of uncertainty on her face. "All right, what do you have?"

She gave him a sheepish grimace. "How about you going first."

He gently squeezed her hand. "How about if we go together? I'll start off and then we'll alternate."

She nodded. "What if we have the same ones?"

"That will be okay. We'll talk about all of them." He picked up his piece of paper. "First on my list is communication."

Sienna smiled ruefully. "It's first on mine, too. And I agree that we need to talk more, without arguing. Not that you argued—I think you would hold stuff in when I made you upset instead of getting it out and speaking your mind."

Dane stared at her for a moment, then a smile touched his lips. "You're right, you know. I always had to plug in the last word and I did it because I knew it would piss you off."

"Well, stop doing it."

He grinned. "Okay. The next time I'll hang around for us to talk through things. But then you're going to have to make sure that you're available when we need to talk. You can't let anything, not even your job, get in the way of us communicating."

"Okay, I agree."

"Now what's next on your list?" he asked.

She looked up at him and smiled. "Patience. I know you said that I don't have patience, but neither do you. But you used to."

Dane shook his head. "Yeah, I lost my patience when you did. I thought to myself, why should I be patient with you when you weren't doing the same with me? Sometimes I think you thought I enjoyed knowing you had a bad day or didn't make a sale, and that wasn't it at all. At some point what was suddenly important to you wasn't important to me anymore."

"And because of it, we both became detached," Sienna said softly.

"Yes, we did." He reached out and lifted her chin. "I promise to do a better job of being patient, Sienna."

"So will I, Dane."

They alternated, going down the list. They had a number of the same things on both lists and they discussed everything in detail, acknowledging their faults and what they could have done to make things better. They also discussed what they would do in the future to strengthen their marriage.

"That's all I have on my list," Dane said a while later. "Do you have anything else?"

Sienna's finger glided over her list. For a short while she thought about pretending she didn't have anything else, but they had agreed to be completely honest. They had definitely done so when they had discussed her spending more time at work than at home.

"So what's the last thing on your list, Sienna? What do you see as one of the things that went wrong with our marriage?"

She lifted her chin and met his gaze and said, "My inability to stand up to your parents."

He looked at her with deep dark eyes. "Okay, then. Let's talk about that."

Seventeen

Dane waited patiently for Sienna to begin talking and gently rubbed the back of her hand while doing so. He'd known the issue of his parents had always been a challenge to her. Over the years he had tried to make her see that how the elder Bradfords felt didn't matter. What he failed to realize, accept and understand was that it *did* matter…to her.

She had grown up in a family without love, so when they married, she not only sought his love, but that of his family. Being accepted meant a lot to her, and her expectations of the Bradfords, given how they operated and their family history, were too high.

They weren't a close-knit bunch, never had been and never would be. His parents had allowed their own parents to decide their future, including who they married. When they had come of age, arranged marriages were the norm within the Bradfords' circle. His father had confided to him one night after indulging in too many drinks that his mother had not been his choice for a wife. That hadn't surprised Dane, nor had it bothered him since he would bet that his father probably hadn't been his mother's choice of a husband, either.

"I don't want to rehash the past, Dane," Sienna finally said softly, looking at the blaze in the fireplace instead of at him. "But something you said earlier tonight has made me think about a lot of things. You love your parents, but you've never hesitated in letting them know when you felt they were wrong, nor have you put up with their crap when it came to me."

She switched her gaze from the fire to him. "The problem is that *I* put up with their crap when it came to me. And you were right. I thought I had to actually prove something to them, show them I was worthy of you and your love, and I've spent the better part of a year and a half doing that, and all it did was bring me closer and closer to losing you. I'm sure they've been walking around with big smiles on their faces since you got the divorce petition. But I refuse to let them be happy at my expense and my own heartbreak."

She scooted closer to Dane and splayed her hands against his chest. "It's time I become more assertive with your parents, Dane. Because it's not about them—it's about us. I refuse to let them make me feel unworthy any longer, because I am worthy to be loved by you. I don't have anything to prove. They either accept me as I am or not at all. The only person who matters anymore is you."

With his gaze holding hers, Dane lifted one of her hands off his chest and brought it to his lips and placed a kiss in the palm. "I'm glad you've finally come to realize that, Sienna. And I wholeheartedly understand and agree. I was made to love you, and if my parents never accept that then it's their loss, not ours."

Tears constricted Sienna's throat and she swallowed deeply before she could find her voice to say, "I love you, Dane. I don't want the divorce. I never did. I want to belong to you and I want you to belong to me. I just want to make you happy."

"And I love you, too, Sienna, and I don't want the divorce,

either. My life will be nothing without you being a part of it. I love you so much, and I've missed you."

And with his heart pounding hard in his chest, he leaned over and captured her lips, intent on showing her just what he meant.

Eighteen

This is homecoming, Sienna thought as she was quickly consumed by the hungry onslaught of Dane's kiss. All the hurt and anger she'd felt for six months was being replaced by passion of the most heated kind. All she could think about was the desire she was feeling being back in the arms of the man she loved and who loved her.

This was the type of communication she'd always loved, where she could share her thoughts, feelings and desires with Dane without uttering a single word. It was where their deepest emotions and what was in their inner hearts spoke for them, expressing things so eloquently and not leaving any room for misunderstandings.

He pulled back slightly, his lips hovering within inches of hers. He reached out and caressed her cheek, and as if she needed his taste again, her lips automatically parted. A slow, sensual acknowledgement of understanding tilted the corners of his mouth into a smile. Then he leaned closer and kissed her again, longer and harder, and the only thing she could do was to wrap her arms around him and silently thank God for reuniting her with this very special man.

Dane was hungry for the taste of his wife and at that moment, as his heart continued to pound relentlessly in his chest, he knew he had to make love to her, to show her in every way what she meant to him, had always meant to him and would always mean to him.

He pulled back slightly and the moisture that was left on her lips made his stomach clench. He leaned forward and licked them dry, or tried to, but her scent was driving him to do more. "Please let me make love to you, Sienna," he whispered, leaning down and resting his forehead against hers.

She leaned back and cupped his chin with her hand. "Oh, yes. I want you to make love to me, Dane. I've missed being with you so much I ache."

"Oh, baby, I love you." He pulled her closer, murmured the words in her twisted locks, kissed her cheek, her temple, her lips, and he cupped her buttocks, practically lifting her off the floor in the process. His breath came out harsh, ragged as the chemistry between them sizzled. There was only one way to drench their fire.

He stretched out with her in front of the fireplace, as he began removing her clothes and then his. Moments later, the blaze from the fire was a flickering light across their naked skin. And then he began kissing her all over, leaving no part of her untouched, determined to quench his hunger and his desire. He had missed the taste of her and was determined to be reacquainted in every way he could think of.

"Dane…"

Her tortured moan ignited the passion within him, and he leaned forward to position his body over hers, letting his throbbing erection come to rest between her thighs, gently touching the entrance of her moist heat. He lifted his head to look down at her, wanting to see her expression the exact moment their bodies joined again.

Nineteen

Sienna stared into Dane's eyes, the heat and passion she saw in them making her shiver. The love she recognized made her heart pound, and the desire she felt for him sent surges and surges of sensations through every part of her body, especially the area between her legs, making her thighs quiver.

"You're my everything, Sienna," he whispered as he began easing inside of her. His gaze was locked with hers as his voice came out in a husky tone. "I need you like I need air to breathe, water for thirst and food for nourishment. Oh, baby, my life has been so empty since you've been gone. I love and need you."

His words touched her, and when he was embedded inside of her to the hilt, she arched her back, needing and wanting even more of him. She gripped his shoulders with her fingers as liquid fire seemed to flow to all parts of her body. And at that moment she forgot everything—the Beast from the East, their limited supply of food and the fact they were stranded together in a cabin with barely enough heat. The only thing that registered in her mind was that they were together and expressing their love in a way that literally touched her soul.

He continued to stroke her, in and out, and with each powerful thrust into her body she moaned out his name and told him of her love. She was like a bow whose strings were being stretched to the limit each and every time he drove into her, and she met his thrusts with her own eager ones.

And then she felt it, the strength like a volcano erupting as he continued to stroke her to oblivion. Her body splintered into a thousand pieces as an orgasm ripped through her, almost snatching her breath away. And when she felt him buck, tighten his hold on her hips and thrust into her deeper, she knew that same powerful sensation had taken hold of him, as well.

"Sienna!"

He screamed her name and growled a couple of words that were incoherent to her ears. She tightened her arms around his neck, needing to be as close to him as she could get. She knew in her heart at that moment that things were going to be fine. She and Dane had proven that when it came to the power of love, it was never too late.

Sienna awoke the following morning naked, in front of the fireplace and cuddled in her husband's arms with a blanket covering them. After yawning, she raised her chin and glanced over at him and met his gaze head-on. The intensity in the dark eyes staring back at her shot heat through all parts of her body. She couldn't help but recall last night and how they had tried making up for all the time they had been apart.

"It's gone," Dane said softly, pulling her closer into his arms.

She lifted a brow. "What's gone?"

"The beast."

She tilted her head to glance out the window and he was right. Although snow was still falling, it wasn't the violent blizzard that had been unleashed the day before. It was as if the weather had served the purpose it had come for and had made its exit. She smiled. Evidently, someone up there knew her and Dane's relationship was meant to be saved and had stepped in to salvage it.

She was about to say something when suddenly there was a loud pounding at the door. She and Dane looked at each other, wondering who would be paying them a visit to the cabin at this hour and in this weather.

Twenty

Sienna, like Dane, had quickly gotten dressed and was now staring at the four men who were standing in the doorway… those handsome Steele brothers. She smiled, shaking her head. Vanessa had evidently called her cousins to come rescue her anyway.

"Vanessa called us," Chance Steele, the oldest of the pack, said by way of explanation. "It just so happened that we were only a couple of miles down the road at our own cabin." A smile touched his lips. "She was concerned that the two of you were here starving to death and asked us to share some of our rations."

"Thanks, guys," Dane said, gladly accepting the box Sebastian Steele was handing him. "Come on in. And although we've had plenty of heat to keep us warm, I have to admit our food supply was kind of low."

As soon as the four entered, all eyes went to Sienna. Although the brothers knew Dane because their families sometimes ran in the same social circles, as well as the fact that

Dane and Donovan Steele had graduated from high school the same year, she knew their main concern was for her. She had been their cousin Vanessa's best friend for years, and as a result they had sort of adopted her as their little cousin, as well.

"You okay?" Morgan Steele asked her, although Sienna knew she had to look fine, probably like a woman who'd been made love to all night, and she wasn't ashamed of that fact. After all, Dane *was* her husband. But the Steeles knew about her pending divorce, so she decided to end their worries.

She smiled and moved closer to Dane. He automatically wrapped his arms around her shoulders and brought her closer to his side. "Yes, I'm wonderful," she said, breaking the subtle tension she felt in the room. "Dane and I have decided we don't want a divorce and intend to stay together and make our marriage work."

The relieved smiles on the faces of the four men were priceless. "That's wonderful. We're happy for you," Donovan Steele said, grinning.

"We apologize if we interrupted anything, but you know Vanessa," Chance said, smiling. "She wouldn't let up. We would have come sooner but the bad weather kept us away."

"Your timing was perfect," Dane said, grinning. "We appreciate you even coming out now. I'm sure the roads weren't their best."

"No, but my new truck managed just fine," Sebastian said proudly. "Besides, we're going fishing later. We would invite you to join us, Dane, but I'm sure you can think of other ways you'd prefer to spend your time."

Dane smiled as he glanced down and met Sienna's gaze. "Oh yeah, I can definitely think of a few."

The power had been restored and a couple of hours later, after eating a hefty breakfast of pancakes, sausage, grits and eggs, and drinking what Dane had to admit was the best coffee he'd had in a long time, Dane and Sienna were wrapped in each other's arms in the king-size bed. Sensations flowed through her just thinking about how they had ached and hungered for each other, and the fierceness of their lovemaking to fulfill that need and greed.

"Now will you tell me what brought you to the cabin?" Sienna asked, turning in Dane's arms and meeting his gaze.

"My wedding band." He then told her why he'd come to the cabin two weeks ago and how he'd left the ring behind. "It was as if without that ring on my finger, my connection to you was gone. I had to have it back so I came here for it."

Sienna nodded, understanding completely. That was one of the reasons she hadn't removed hers. Reaching out she cupped his stubbled jaw in her hand and then leaned over and kissed him softly. "Together forever, Mr. Bradford."

Dane smiled. "Yes, Mrs. Bradford, together forever. We've proven that when it comes to true love, it's never too late."

* * * * *

PASSION

Harlequin® *Desire*

COMING NEXT MONTH
AVAILABLE APRIL 10, 2012

#2149 FEELING THE HEAT
The Westmorelands
Brenda Jackson
Dr. Micah Westmoreland knows Kalina Daniels hasn't forgiven him. But he can't ignore the heat that still burns between them....

#2150 ON THE VERGE OF I DO
Dynasties: The Kincaids
Heidi Betts

#2151 HONORABLE INTENTIONS
Billionaires and Babies
Catherine Mann

#2152 WHAT LIES BENEATH
Andrea Laurence

#2153 UNFINISHED BUSINESS
Cat Schield

#2154 A BREATHLESS BRIDE
The Pearl House
Fiona Brand

REQUEST YOUR FREE BOOKS!
2 FREE NOVELS PLUS 2 FREE GIFTS!

Harlequin® Desire

ALWAYS POWERFUL, PASSIONATE AND PROVOCATIVE

YES! Please send me 2 FREE Harlequin Desire® novels and my 2 FREE gifts (gifts are worth about $10). After receiving them, if I don't wish to receive any more books, I can return the shipping statement marked "cancel." If I don't cancel, I will receive 6 brand-new novels every month and be billed just $4.30 per book in the U.S. or $4.99 per book in Canada. That's a saving of at least 14% off the cover price! It's quite a bargain! Shipping and handling is just 50¢ per book in the U.S. and 75¢ per book in Canada.* I understand that accepting the 2 free books and gifts places me under no obligation to buy anything. I can always return a shipment and cancel at any time. Even if I never buy another book, the two free books and gifts are mine to keep forever.

225/326 HDN FEF3

Name _____ (PLEASE PRINT) _____

Address _____ Apt. #

City _____ State/Prov. _____ Zip/Postal Code

Signature (if under 18, a parent or guardian must sign)

Mail to the **Reader Service:**
IN U.S.A.: P.O. Box 1867, Buffalo, NY 14240-1867
IN CANADA: P.O. Box 609, Fort Erie, Ontario L2A 5X3

Not valid for current subscribers to Harlequin Desire books.

Want to try two free books from another line?
Call 1-800-873-8635 or visit www.ReaderService.com.

* Terms and prices subject to change without notice. Prices do not include applicable taxes. Sales tax applicable in N.Y. Canadian residents will be charged applicable taxes. Offer not valid in Quebec. This offer is limited to one order per household. All orders subject to credit approval. Credit or debit balances in a customer's account(s) may be offset by any other outstanding balance owed by or to the customer. Please allow 4 to 6 weeks for delivery. Offer available while quantities last.

Your Privacy—The Reader Service is committed to protecting your privacy. Our Privacy Policy is available online at www.ReaderService.com or upon request from the Reader Service.

We make a portion of our mailing list available to reputable third parties that offer products we believe may interest you. If you prefer that we not exchange your name with third parties, or if you wish to clarify or modify your communication preferences, please visit us at www.ReaderService.com/consumerchoice or write to us at Reader Service Preference Service, P.O. Box 9062, Buffalo, NY 14269. Include your complete name and address.

HDES11B

Harlequin® *Blaze*™
red-hot reads

**Sizzling fairy tales
to make every fantasy come true!**

Fan-favorite authors
Tori Carrington and Kate Hoffmann
bring readers

Blazing Bedtime Stories, Volume VI

MAID FOR HIM...

Successful businessman Kieran Morrison doesn't dare hope for
a big catch when he goes fishing. But when he wakes up one
night to find a beautiful woman seemingly unconscious on the
deck of his sailboat, he lands one bigger than he could ever
have imagined by way of mermaid Daphne Moore.
But is she real? Or just a fantasy?

OFF THE BEATEN PATH

Greta Adler and Alex Hansen have been friends for seven years.
So when Greta agrees to accompany Alex at a mountain retreat
owned by a client, she doesn't realize that Alex has a different
path he wants their relationshiop to take.
But will Greta follow his lead?

Available April 2012 wherever books are sold.

Taft Bowman knew he'd ruined any chance he'd had for happiness with Laura Pendleton when he drove her away years ago...and into the arms of another man, thousands of miles away. Now she was back, a widow with two small children...and despite himself, he was starting to believe in second chances.

Harlequin Special® Edition® presents a new installment in USA TODAY bestselling author RaeAnne Thayne's miniseries,
THE COWBOYS OF COLD CREEK.

Enjoy a sneak peek of
A COLD CREEK REUNION

Available April 2012 from Harlequin® Special Edition®

A younger woman stood there, and from this distance he had only a strange impression, as though she was somehow standing on an island of calm amid the chaos of the scene, the flashing lights of the emergency vehicles, shouts between his crew members, the excited buzz of the crowd.

And then the woman turned and he just about tripped over a snaking fire hose somebody shouldn't have left there.

Laura.

He froze, and for the first time in fifteen years as a firefighter, he forgot about the incident, his mission, just what the hell he was doing here.

Laura.

Ten years. He hadn't seen her in all that time, since the week before their wedding when she had given him back his ring and left town. Not just town. She had left the whole damn country, as if she couldn't run far enough to get away from him.

Some part of him desperately wanted to think he had made some kind of mistake. It couldn't be her. That was just some other slender woman with a long sweep of honey-blond hair and big, blue, unforgettable eyes. But no. It was definitely Laura. Sweet and lovely.

Not his.

He was going to have to go over there and talk to her. He didn't want to. He wanted to stand there and pretend he hadn't seen her. But he was the fire chief. He couldn't hide out just because he had a painful history with the daughter of the property owner.

Sometimes he hated his job.

Will Taft and Laura be able to make the years recede...or is the gulf between them too broad to ever cross?

Find out in
A COLD CREEK REUNION
Available April 2012 from Harlequin® Special Edition®
wherever books are sold.

Celebrate the 30th anniversary
of Harlequin® Special Edition® with a bonus story
included in each Special Edition® book in April!